His Voice Was like Dark Velvet.

"Laura," he murmured, "when I found you in the garden you were looking at the new shoots coming up out of the ground. You know, they don't have to worry about what they're doing. They just react automatically to the sun warming the cold earth." As he spoke, his fingers moved down her neck to her shoulders, sending sensual messages through her body.

"But it's not that simple for people, is it?" he continued. "We have to think, analyze, examine motives. How much easier it would be if we could simply trust ourselves to respond to our feelings."

"It's not just trusting ourselves," she whispered. "It's trusting other people."

"I know. And I'll give you the time for that. I promise."

AMANDA LEE

lives in Maryland and is a wife and mother, as well as an author of fiction and nonfiction. A woman of many talents, she particularly enjoys writing about two of life's greatest pleasures—romance and food. Her lively sense of humor is evident in the sparkling dialogue of her characters.

Dear Reader:

SILHOUETTE DESIRE is an exciting new line of contemporary romances from Silhouette Books. During the past year, many Silhouette readers have written in telling us what other types of stories they'd like to read from Silhouette, and we've kept these comments and suggestions in mind in developing SILHOUETTE DESIRE.

DESIREs feature all of the elements you like to see in a romance, plus a more sensual, provocative story. So if you want to experience all the excitement, passion and joy of falling in love, then SILHOUETTE DESIRE is for you.

Karen Solem
Editor-in-Chief
Silhouette Books

AMANDA LEE
More Than Promises

Silhouette Desire

Published by Silhouette Books New York

America's Publisher of Contemporary Romance

Silhouette Books by Amanda Lee

SILHOUETTE BOOKS
300 E. 42nd St., New York, N.Y. 10017

Copyright © 1985 by Ruth Glick
Cover artwork copyright © 1985 Howard Rogers Inc.

Distributed by Pocket Books

ISBN: 0-373-05192-1

First Silhouette Books printing February, 1985

10 9 8 7 6 5 4 3 2 1

America's Publisher of Contemporary Romance

Printed in the U.S.A.

More Than Promises

1

~~~~~~~~~~

The March wind played tag with Laura Carson all the way across the parking lot and then gave her a little push inside the front entrance of the garden center. Wishing that she'd worn a heavier jacket, the slender young woman shivered as she turned and tried to secure the door of the converted barn.

What a morning to be selling garden furniture and bedding stock, she thought wryly. It seemed highly unlikely that she'd be doing much business until the weather settled down a bit.

Wondering why she'd even bothered to open on time, Laura smoothed her wind-tossed hair with a few quick strokes and then headed for the back room to hang up her coat. In fact, she was so certain there would be no business that when the phone rang at precisely 10 A.M., she jumped and then grinned at her startled reaction before picking up the receiver.

"Hello. Carson's. May I help you?" she inquired.

There was a moment's hesitation, and then a male

voice began, "Uh, yes, I'd like some information about your landscape design service." The voice was mellow in timbre, and yet it had an intriguing, scratchy underlayer, as though it were equal parts finely polished leather and sandpaper.

It took Laura a second to answer. The man on the other end of the line had spoken only one brief sentence. And yet, for her, there was something so compelling about the sound that it was hard to focus on his words. "What would you like to know?" she finally managed.

"I've just moved to Maryland, and Carson's has been strongly recommended. What type of services do you offer?"

"Quite a full range," Laura began, and then ran quickly through the list, glad that she could rattle it off by heart.

"Do you provide all the construction materials and the plants, as well as a work crew?"

"We can work that way. Then all the plants are guaranteed by our replacement policy. Or, if you want to supply some of the nursery stock or materials yourself, we can also work on that basis."

A number of other questions followed, all of which Laura did her best to answer succinctly, but it was impossible for her not to sound a bit enthusiastic about what Carson's had to offer. After all, she had developed many of the services herself.

"Well, it certainly seems as though you have what I'm looking for."

Was she imagining it, or had his tone suddenly become a lot warmer? Laura wondered.

"When can I make an appointment?" he was saying.

"You can stop in anytime. We're open until five through March thirty-first and after that until nine P.M.," she returned, struggling to sound matter-of-fact. There was a good chance, she reminded herself, that this was going to be her last contact with the man on the other end of the phone line. Prospective customers who called out of the blue were as likely to change their minds as to actually stop by—even if they *had* an appointment.

"Yes, well then, tell your boss Brandon McGuire will be in to talk with him later."

"My boss?" Laura sputtered. "I am . . ." But he had already said goodbye and hung up. My boss, she thought. Of all the nerve.

For a moment she stood staring wordlessly at the receiver before replacing it carefully in its cradle. Then she shook her head and sighed. If she was piqued at the man who had identified himself as Brandon McGuire, it was as much from her oddly out-of-proportion reaction to his vocal delivery as to his casual assumption that the resident landscape architect at Carson's was a man. But that wasn't playing fair. How could she expect him to know her professional status from their brief exchange? And what if he'd come in and found her standing here behind the front counter in her faded jeans and an old navy turtleneck? For a moment she pictured how she must look, with the blue eyes that her father had always called "innocent" and her dark hair feathered casually back from her face—and probably still mussed from the wind. No, if Mr. McGuire had walked in the door instead of phoning, he might well have made the same mistake.

Suddenly she felt the urge to rush back to the workroom so she could put on some lipstick and run a comb through her hair. Maybe that would make her look a bit more in charge. But she stifled the impulse. This was ridiculous. She didn't have to prove anything to a voice over the phone. She knew who she was and what she was doing here.

For a moment, Laura permitted herself an appreciative glance around the beautifully converted barn that housed Carson's. Forty years ago when her parents had set up shop here, the property had been dilapidated. But the Harperstown suburbs had moved out to meet them, and the establishment had prospered. When her father's health had forced the couple to move to New Mexico, they had turned the whole thing over to Laura. And in her capable hands, the business was doing better than ever.

Laura's reflections were interrupted as the door flew open and Gary Gorman, her co-op student from the community college, blew inside.

"Hi. I see the wind's still at it," she greeted him cheerfully, wondering once again why he chose to wear wire-rimmed spectacles that made him look more like a colonial shopkeeper than a modern-day teenager. But she would never embarrass him by making the observation.

"Why don't you warm up with a cup of coffee before we start setting out the early annuals," she added, crossing to the greenhouse that had been added along one long wall of the building. Pushing open the door, she stopped for a moment to appreciate the rich, fertile bouquet of the air. It smelled of plants and soil and possibilities—for Laura was rarely able to handle bedding stock without finding her mind spinning off into the future. She was mentally planting impatiens around the deck she was designing for the Simpsons when Gary reappeared, coffee cup in hand.

"Let's put the plants with the most flowers at the front of the tables," she directed. "I'll sort the geraniums by color. You do the begonias."

As usual, Laura worked silently and efficiently. But today Gary would have been surprised to learn how quickly her mind wandered from its accustomed paths. She had barely arranged half the white geraniums when she found herself thinking not of color and texture of foliage, but of Brandon McGuire—a voice with a very different kind of texture and color.

What did he look like? she wondered, trying to conjure up a picture of the man. It was an impulse, she realized, that she had been fighting almost since she put the phone down. And finally she simply had to give in to it.

He was probably tall, she speculated. And he had to

have dark hair—and dark eyes. She just couldn't imagine a blue-eyed blond producing that combination of gravel and richness. She grinned at her own cleverness and then went on to fill in more details.

For some reason, she saw him dressed in a conservatively tailored business suit—gray, with a subtly striped shirt. The only touch of color was his burgundy tie.

"Hey," Gary broke into her thoughts, "you look as though your mind's a million miles away."

To her embarrassment, Laura flushed, feeling suddenly like a kid caught snitching a taste of icing from a cake. It had been a long time since she'd let such detailed speculations about a man occupy her thoughts—and a man she'd never even met, at that. The realization was surprising and more than a bit disturbing. And all at once she found herself feeling irrationally irritated with Mr. Brandon McGuire, whoever he was.

"I'll bet you were making plans for those geraniums," Gary surmised, unaware of her conflicting emotions.

His employer ducked down to get another flat of flowers. "Could be," she allowed, and then changed the subject. "Listen, why don't you finish up here and then go pick up the seed packets and potting soil that arrived at the depot yesterday evening," she suggested. "I think I'll try to set up the display of budget garden furniture I've been avoiding all week."

Before departing, Gary brought two cartons containing an unassembled chair and chaise longue from the crowded back room. Laura had planned to tackle them outside. But that was impossible today. The pieces would certainly blow away before she got the things put together.

Where was she going to work? she wondered, looking around at the aisles of planters, fertilizer, potting soil and garden books. And then the two-level wooden display deck in the center of the store caught her eye. It was decorated with tropical plants and a wrought-iron table and chairs. But they could easily be pushed to the side.

11

Fifteen minutes later she was sitting in the middle of the deck staring at a set of instructions that were obviously designed for professional engineers. As far as she could tell, the chaise longue had to be assembled upside down and backwards. And it had either too many legs or too few arms.

Laura was so intent on sorting out the various nuts and bolts and trying to determine which of three almost identical pieces of aluminum tubing was actually the "center support brace," that she didn't hear the door open. Nor was she aware of well-cushioned jogging shoes coming up the aisle toward the deck.

The owner of the shoes stopped next to a display of hand tools and looked at her quizzically, taking in the soft wing of raven hair that now fell across her forehead, the slender neck bent in concentration, and the faded blue jeans she wore. He found the effect charming—and a bit perplexing.

This casually dressed girl seemed to be the only person around. Could she possibly be the same woman he had talked to on the phone at ten? Her voice, with its combination of sophistication and breathiness, was the sexiest thing he had heard in ages, and yet he somehow knew instinctively that it was not put on. That voice had almost made him forget what he had called about. And he cursed himself for not having gotten her name.

But name or no, she had been invading his thoughts all morning while he struggled to keep his mind on administrative staff requirements, heating plants and expected annual occupancy rates. Finally he had given up, switched off his computer terminal and driven over to Carson's.

While he hesitated beside the trowels and cutting shears, he saw the girl he had been so thoughtfully watching drop a washer.

He smiled at her mumbled expletive as the little metal wheel rolled along one of the wide deck boards and then dropped through to the brick floor below. She was reaching through to try to retrieve it when her long, tapered hand brushed against the rough wood, and he heard a little exclamation of pain. And suddenly he was rushing forward.

"What happened . . . ?" he began.

But the look of surprise in her wide blue eyes made him halt. They were the deepest blue he had ever seen, the color of Alpine lakes.

"I'm sorry. I didn't mean to sneak up on you. There wasn't anyone at the front desk, and the door was open," he found himself pointing out stupidly. "And then you were so absorbed with whatever it is you're trying to put together."

He had thought the explanation would be sufficient. But she kept staring at him so oddly. He saw her purse her rather full lips.

"Brandon McGuire," she finally said. Somehow she had forgotten completely that she was supposed to be irritated with the man.

Her voice brought a smile of recognition to his lips. So she was the one! She didn't have quite the same sophisticated tone in person as over the phone, he noted. You couldn't see her speak and get exactly the same impression—probably because she looked so damn young.

"To see the landscape architect," he reminded her, the rough quality in his voice suddenly more apparent. It was like the undertow of an ocean wave now, rushing backwards over the sand, pulling everything it could carry back to the sea.

"Yes. Well, you're seeing her," Laura informed him as calmly as possible. At the same time she started to push herself up from the deck.

"You're the—?" he began.

But he was cut off instantly by her wince of pain as the splinter she had forgotten pressed suddenly against the hard surface of the deck.

"Let me see that," he demanded, closing the remaining distance between them in a few quick strides. For a moment he seemed to tower over her, and then he leaned down to take her by the elbows and help her up.

"Really, I can manage," Laura tried to protest. But he had already seized her right hand and was beginning to unfold it gently. There was no way she could suppress a little shiver of awareness at the contact of his warm flesh against hers. Had he noticed? she wondered.

His next words implied that the focus of his attention was elsewhere. "There's quite a wicked-looking sliver in your little finger," he informed her gravely. "But I think I can get it if you hold still."

As she watched, he tried to grasp the protruding piece of wood with the closely trimmed nails of his thumb and index finger. But it was simply too short.

"Damn," he swore under his breath.

Before she could utter a protest, he was turning her hand and lifting it quickly to his lips. Mesmerized, she watched him grasp the splinter's end between square white teeth, vividly aware of their controlled pressure against her skin. And then with swift movement, he had pulled the splinter out.

Still holding her hand captive in one of his, he reached up with the other to remove the little sliver of wood from his mouth.

Their eyes met then, and she saw a mischievous grin playing around the corners of his lips. "I saw that done in an old John Wayne movie," he informed her gravely. "Only it was a bullet in the shoulder, not a splinter in the finger."

Laura stared at him for a moment. "Yes, well, thanks a lot, stranger," she answered, affecting a Western drawl that matched the lightness of his tone. At the same time she disengaged her hand.

Pretending to inspect the recent wound, she gazed up at her benefactor surreptitiously from under lowered lashes. She was trying to reconcile the flesh-and-blood man with the fantasy she'd built up about him. She

14

certainly hadn't been prepared for his slightly offbeat sense of humor. But she had guessed right about the dark eyes—and the dark hair. The latter had the merest hint of a natural wave. His brows, too, were dark and thick. His lips were not as full as she had imagined. And he was not quite so tall as she had assumed. But his chest was broad, she noted, as her eyes swept across the off-white fisherman's knit sweater he was wearing under his rain slicker. Letting her gaze drop lower, she saw that he was clad in well-worn jeans and expensive jogging shoes. The discovery made her smile broadly. She had definitely been wrong about his attire.

"Are you laughing at my primitive surgical technique?"

"What?" Laura was momentarily disoriented by the question. She had forgotten that she had been pretending a deep interest in her injured finger.

"Are you amused at my method of splinter removal?" he asked, rephrasing the query.

"No, your clothing," she blurted, and then clapped her hand to her mouth as she realized what she had said.

"I beg your pardon? I know these jeans are old, but I don't believe any of the seams are split."

"Oh, no. I didn't mean . . ." Laura began.

He cocked a shaggy eyebrow.

"It's just that when I pictured you after our phone conversation this morning, I dressed you in a gray flannel suit. So I wasn't making fun of you. I was thinking about how far off I was." Laura stopped abruptly. Why in the world was she babbling on like this? And why was she letting this man know that he'd occupied her thoughts after they'd hung up the phone?

"It's okay. I made the same mistake," he admitted.

It was Laura's turn to look quizzical.

"I didn't imagine you dressed so casually, either," he clarified. "And I thought you must be a bit more . . ." He paused, searching for the right word, and finally added, "Mature. Are you sure you're old enough to be a certified landscape architect?"

Laura drew herself up to her full five feet three inches. "I earned my master's degree four years ago," she informed him, unable to keep a note of pride out of her voice. "I've been the owner of Carson's Garden Center for the past two years, and I've been running the place for almost twice that long. Does that background fit your specifications?"

At her words, he took a step backwards. "Don't shoot, ma'am," he pleaded, raising his hands in mock surrender. "I certainly didn't mean to impugn your professional reputation."

Laura couldn't stifle a grin. "I'm sorry. It's just that—"

"It's just that we've somehow gotten off on the wrong foot," he finished for her. "Let's call a truce and start all over again. I'm Brandon McGuire." As he spoke he held out his hand.

"Laura Carson," she answered, automatically clasping his hand. Just as when he'd touched her before, she was suddenly vividly aware of the strength of his grasp and the encompassing warmth of his large fingers.

"What can I do for you, Mr. McGuire?" she asked as lightly as possible.

She saw an unspoken answer to her question in the warmth of his look.

"Brandon," he corrected. "Call me Brandon. I'm interested in some rather extensive outdoor construction and landscaping."

"For an office building? An estate? An apartment complex?" she asked, glad to be able to enter a realm where she had control of the situation.

He grinned. "If you put it that way, I guess it's not so extensive. It's for a house."

"Modern or traditional?"

"Oh, very modern. You may know the place. It's out on the Littlefield Road about three-quarters of the way up the hill overlooking the river valley."

Laura nodded, all business now. "That house Jim Fitzgerald built on speculation earlier this year?"

"Yes. I was lucky to find it."

"I think you're right," Laura acknowledged, remembering the property in question. The house was a real luxury production—too rich for the area, she had thought as she'd watched the construction progress. Wheels were already beginning to spin in her head as she remembered the unusual lay of the land. The steep slope would be a challenge to landscape and would lend itself to some unusual treatments.

"I suppose you have pictures of some of your previous projects that I could look at," Brandon was saying.

"Of course. Come on back to my office." Laura turned and led the way toward the back of the barn. Ushering her visitor into a small but cozy room, she pointed to a Windsor chair in the corner by the window and several leather-bound albums.

"Why don't you look through some of those," she suggested, "while I get a little paper work done."

"Fine."

Brandon studied the color photographs of assorted gardens and outdoor structures with interest, noting the attention to detail, the artful placement of flowers and shrubbery, the way the construction had been adapted to the terrain. He hadn't known exactly what to expect when he'd opened the books, but now he could see that Laura Carson had every right to be proud of her achievements. She might look like a kid, but her work definitely ranked her at the top of her field.

One of her gardens in particular caught his attention. It had obviously been designed to make the most of a small space. Its focus was a rather large free-form fish pond bisected with a humpback wooden bridge. It had taken considerable skill, he realized, to make the large pond work in the tiny garden. And yet it all looked quite natural, almost as if she had simply incorporated an existing feature into her design.

Glancing up across the room at the remarkable woman who had pulled that off, he caught her looking at him instead of at the papers she had mentioned. And from the intensity of her expression, he could see that she was waiting for a verdict. Did she always care how people reacted to her work? he wondered. Or was there something special about her response to him? He couldn't help hoping it was the latter.

"These are charming," he pronounced.

"Thank you."

"You pour a lot of yourself into these projects, don't you?"

"Yes." In a way, they're like my children, she added silently. The children I'll never have. But those painful, final words went unspoken. In fact, Laura wasn't even conscious of having called up the thought behind them, so much was it a part of the fabric of her existence. It wasn't a sharp pain anymore, just a dull, remembered ache from an old psychic injury that had never properly healed.

But the man who sat opposite her noticed its effect. His contact with this woman had been brief. But somehow he had found himself strangely attuned to her. He knew it was because he recognized an affinity between them, and also because he was attracted to her—more attracted than he had been to anyone in a long, long time.

It was impossible not to sense that the attraction was returned. Yet he could also detect a reluctance, a wariness about her. It was as though she kept veiling her natural responses to him.

Why? he asked himself, studying her face for some further clue. If he had to guess, he'd say that someone had hurt Laura Carson very badly in the past, and that she was afraid of getting hurt again. He couldn't know precisely what had happened to her. But he recognized her guarded, protective manner. He had relied on something quite similar in the not too distant past. And he understood it quite well.

His speculation was cut off by her question. "Why

18

don't you tell me a little bit more about the kind of project you have in mind," she asked in a very businesslike voice as she reached in her desk for a pad of paper and pencil.

"I've got a better idea. Why don't I drive you over to my place so you can have a look around," he suggested, his smile direct and engaging.

"Oh, I couldn't possibly do that," she answered, drawing back slightly.

"Why not?"

"Well, I haven't actually accepted the commission," she began.

"But you will."

"Yes," she acknowledged, dropping the pretense that she might not do the work for him. The job he had offered her was just too tempting.

"But I *am* afraid I can't come out this morning—since I'm alone in the garden center," she added.

Brandon nodded. "This afternoon then?"

She was about to propose an appointment later in the week when she changed her mind. Her second-in-command, Sylvia Gordon, would be in after lunch. So why not get this consultation over with? "All right. How about three o'clock?" she asked.

"If that's the earliest you can work me in," he replied amiably, setting down her albums on the table and getting to his feet. "Until this afternoon, then," he added, turning toward the door.

His departure had the same sort of abruptness as the end of his phone call, she realized. To Laura it was an indication that Mr. McGuire knew exactly what he wanted and how to get it with the least amount of wasted motion.

To her annoyance, the realization made her shiver slightly. What was it about the man that made her so wary? Laura asked herself. She already knew the answer. For one thing, she was attracted to him, more attracted than she had been to anyone since—Arthur. She hadn't thought about her former fiancé for a long time. Now she shook her head as if the gesture could dispel all the hurtful memories. She had promised herself she was never going to open herself up to that kind of pain and rejection again. And thus far, keeping that promise hadn't been all that difficult.

So why was she getting so worked up over her reaction to Brandon McGuire? But she knew the answer to that question, too. It wasn't just *her* reaction to *him*. Almost since he'd first walked in, she had gotten the impression that he wanted something more from her than just her professional services. And she had the distinct feeling it was something she was not prepared to give.

Laura got up, crossed to the window and looked out at the well-tended grounds surrounding Carson's. Absent-mindedly she ran her finger along the edge of the mini-blinds, pressing down each narrow metal slat and then letting it spring back into place again with a little ping.

What's gotten into you, she asked herself. Brandon McGuire hasn't even asked you for a date. And if he does, you certainly don't have to accept. You're the one who calls the shots in this situation, not he.

The little pep talk was apparently what she needed. For the rest of the morning she busied herself with the account books and the few customers who stopped in. By lunchtime, she was wondering why she had let herself become so unglued over a simple professional consultation.

That afternoon, as she set out for Brandon McGuire's house, she was almost looking forward to the visit. Half an hour later Laura nosed her small truck up the practically vertical drive. At the summit she found herself in a square gravel area where a blue and white Dodge Blazer was parked.

Laura grinned. Apparently the owner of this property had learned the realities of his precipitous access road. After grabbing her sketch pad, Laura started for the set of mahogany doors at the front entrance. But before she reached them, she stopped. It would probably be less distracting, she told herself, to have a look around alone. She turned and walked to the far edge of the parking area and sat down on a boulder. Glad that the wind had died down enough for her to work, she began to make a sketch of the front elevation and grounds. From this angle, the brick and cedar house appeared to be only one story. But Laura knew that there were at least two more levels built into the back of the hill.

After finishing her first sketch, she got up and walked around to the side of the house. The mulch-covered slope was steeper than she had realized, and for a moment she thought about abandoning the attempt to climb down. But she did need a view of the back.

Gingerly she started down the bank, one hand pressing against the cement foundation. But there was no way she could steady herself. Before she had covered a quarter of the slope, her right foot slid against a loose rock. With a little cry of surprise she landed on her bottom. And then she was shooting down the slope like a kid on a slick metal playground slide. Dropping her note pad, she reached frantically for some handhold to stop her accelerating downward progress. But the construction crew had been all too thorough. There was absolutely nothing to grab.

2

Twisting frantically to the side, Laura tried again to find a handhold. But there was still no way to stop her frightening progress. A picture of herself tumbling all the way down to Littlefield Road flashed into her mind, sending a wave of panic through her nervous system.

However, before she had slid more than a few additional yards, she heard a noise at the back of the house and then Brandon McGuire was stepping around the corner. A smile of welcome curved his well-shaped lips. But it froze as he took in the situation, seeing that she was not coming toward him slowly under her own power but hurtling like an out-of-control bobsledder down the slippery hill. Luckily he had the presence of mind and the reflexes to act quickly. Leaning forward, he pulled her off the slope and several paces onto the flat cement pad by the rear door.

His arms were around her then, pulling her reassuringly against his hard frame. For a moment he simply held her like a child who had taken a bad tumble and needed comforting.

"You're all right; everything's all right now," Brandon murmured, his arms folding her close and his hands stroking her back as she struggled to catch her breath. The words seemed as much a reassurance to himself as to Laura.

She didn't know at first how tightly she was clutching his shoulders. It had been so long since she'd been held in a man's arms. Yet it felt so right, so safe.

Gradually, however, as her fear of the near accident subsided, she became aware of the way she had unconsciously attached herself to his body. She could feel the soft flannel of his shirt against her cheek, and under it, the muscle and sinew of his chest. Even more disturbing were his blue-jean-clad legs, pressed so tightly against hers that she didn't know where she stopped and he began.

Vivid awareness of the intimacy of their position made her draw back. Looking up, she found herself staring into the ebony depths of Brandon's eyes.

"Did I hurt your arm?" he asked, the roughness in his voice dominating, as it seemed to when his emotions were involved. "What were you trying to do, scare the daylights out of me?"

"I—I didn't want to bother you . . ." she began, feeling like a fool.

Brandon raised an eyebrow. "What do you mean? I thought we had an appointment." As he finished speaking, he turned to look at her sketch pad, which lay several paces out on the steep incline. "I suppose you have some valuable drawings and notes in that?" he asked.

"It has preliminary plans for several new projects," she admitted.

"Then I guess I'd better get it for you," he offered. "You've got to know how to walk on this stuff if you don't want to fall down," he added, gesturing toward the mulch.

Without another word, he stepped off the cement slab and started forward to retrieve the note pad. But before he had taken two paces, his feet slid out from under him just as hers had done. Only by grabbing quickly at the metal support pole of the balcony was he able to keep from tumbling down the hill. But he couldn't save himself from coming down heavily and quite unceremoniously on his seat.

For several seconds, Brandon sat silently on the spongy dark mulch. Then he swiveled to face Laura. She waited, not knowing what to expect. Anger, she supposed. Probably directed at her for having gotten him into this situation.

There was no way she could have anticipated the wry amusement that crinkled the skin around his eyes. "As I just said, it takes an expert to be able to fall down in this stuff without hurting himself."

She lost the battle to suppress her own answering grin. Suddenly they were both laughing, sharing the joke as only two veterans of the same campaign can.

Laura forced herself to quit first, wondering if she had bruised his dignity.

"Don't stop," he urged. "I like the way you look when you laugh like that. You ought to try it more often."

"What makes you think I don't?" she shot back.

But he was way ahead of her. He had come to recognize that warning edge in her voice. Take it slow, he admonished himself. Keep it light. She doesn't trust you yet.

Casually he changed the subject back to his own buffoonery. "You know, I really did think I could walk on this stuff without doing a Woody Allen routine," he pointed out. As he spoke, he started to stand up and then apparently reconsidered. "The heck with it. The time for decorum has passed."

To Laura's amazement, he turned his back to her and pushed himself up on all fours before inching a bit farther out onto the ground cover to retrieve her pad.

"Now comes the tricky part," he announced. "Do you have any suggestions on how I might get back to the patio—without calling out the rescue squad?"

"You could crawl," Laura suggested, finding that she was enjoying his predicament more than she should.

"You wouldn't make me do that, would you?" he questioned. "Not after I almost broke my neck rescuing your property." As if for emphasis, he tossed the sketch pad to safety.

Laura shook her head, managing to look contrite. That really wouldn't be very chivalrous of her.

"Then hold on to the balcony brace and give me your hand."

"You don't expect me to pull you back? The most I ever hoist is a twenty-five pound bag of potting soil from time to time."

"I don't expect you to throw me over my shoulder. Just lend me some support."

Laura grabbed the balcony brace with her right hand and reached out to Brandon with her left. She felt her fingers brush his. Inching forward, he clasped her hand more securely. For a moment he simply held on to her so that all her attention became focused on their two sets of fingers grasping each other with a fierce intensity of purpose. She opened her mouth to speak, wondering what she was going to say. Before any words could form, he was pushing himself off the ground with his other hand.

"Pull," he instructed. Laura did, for all she was worth. And his forward momentum almost knocked her off her feet. Reaching out a hand, he grasped her shoulder to steady her.

"Thanks," they both said at once, and then both grinned again.

Laura saw Brandon's gaze inspect the place where he had touched her shoulder and then travel to his hands.

"Now that we look like refugees from a soap commercial, what would you suggest?" he asked.

She shrugged.

"If I knew you better, I'd propose a shower."

"A shower?"

"Yes, you know . . . you go into the bathroom, take off your clothes and let hot water run on your body."

It was a most prosaic and accurate description. Yet she could feel the words making her cheeks redden. It sounded as though he were recommending a joint activity.

"Oh, I meant in complete privacy, of course," he added quickly, catching the skepticism in her eyes.

"Yes, well, thanks, but I believe I'll wait until I get home." As she spoke, she took a step backwards.

"You don't mean you're leaving right now, do you? Didn't you just get here?"

"Actually . . ." she began.

"Actually," he took over quickly, "there's no way to get off the patio without going through the house—or tackling that hill again." He paused to let that bit of information sink in and then continued. "So unless we want to treat my pristine interior decor to a layer of . . ." He plucked a dark shred off Laura's shoulder and held it up. "What, exactly, do you call this stuff, anyway?"

"Shredded root mulch."

"We'd better try to get the shredded root mulch off," Brandon finished. Leaning down, he began to brush industriously at his knees, intent on hiding the slightly wicked gleam in his eyes.

Laura was imitating his example with the splotch on her jacket when she saw him straighten. In the next second she felt his hand swatting back and forth across the seat of her pants.

"Just what do you think you're doing?" she choked out. She would have jumped away, but he grabbed her firmly by the shoulder.

"If you could see your pants, you wouldn't ask. Now hold still and I'll be done in a minute."

Laura closed her eyes. She didn't want to analyze the flutters of awareness he was creating with the stroke of his hand against her bottom.

"Not too hard, is it?" he questioned.

"No." He was holding her arm much too firmly for her to wrest herself away. And she didn't want to make a scene, after all.

"Okay, you'd better do me," he directed when he had finished the job to his satisfaction.

"Do you?"

"I went down on my seat too," he reminded her. "Retrieving *your* note pad."

Laura opened her mouth to refuse and then closed it again. The mulch on his pants *was* her fault. Yet somehow she knew that with another man she would have been able to avoid getting physically involved like this.

"Okay, turn around," she sighed. When he did, Laura found herself staring at the seat of a well-worn pair of jeans. But it wasn't the fabric that held her attention. Much more compelling was the firm swell of the male buttocks that now confronted her—just like in a TV blue-jeans ad. Only this was no male model proudly displaying a close-up of his buns for the camera. It was the all-too-attractive Brandon McGuire, in living 3-D.

"What are you waiting for?" he asked.

"Nothing." Leaning down, she took a tentative swipe at his bottom, and then another, watching with interest as her hand stirred up a little cloud of dark mulch. She tried to pretend she was simply swatting a dirty sofa cushion. But it was no good. She knew precisely how familiarly she was touching him.

She wasn't aware how hard she was swatting until she heard his "Ouch!"

"Oh, sorry," she apologized. "But I think the job's just about done."

"Lucky for me. If you'd gotten any more enthusiastic, I might have had to enjoy the rest of your visit standing up."

"Listen," Laura began, "if you'd rather do this some other time . . ."

"No, I think once is enough."

He turned to face her, grinning for a moment before his expression became more serious. "Actually, I've been looking forward to your coming out here ever since I left the garden center this morning. Don't go away until we have a chance to get some things settled."

For a moment his obsidian eyes locked with her blue ones before she looked down, breaking the contact. That he had admitted anticipating this interview was oddly pleasing, although she couldn't quite admit that to herself.

It was two short flights of stairs up to the main floor. When they reached it, Laura turned to her host in surprise. The living room, with its bare white walls, cathedral ceiling and wide board oak floor, was completely devoid of furnishings. The dining room contained only a card table and two folding chairs.

"Just what exactly were you afraid I was going to get dirty?" she questioned dryly.

Brandon looked around at the almost empty rooms. "You can't say this place isn't pristine," he argued. "Besides, you know how white picks up dirt."

Laura rolled her eyes. But her host already had his hand on her arm and was leading her toward the large windows that made up one wall of the living room.

"Come see the view that persuaded me to buy this place," he suggested. Opening the sliding panel, he ushered her out onto the small deck.

She walked across the wide pine boards and then stood for a moment at the railing, drinking in the panoramic sweep of the gorge below with its dark green pines, rocky outcroppings and rushing water. She had viewed this wild and beautiful valley many times, from dozens of different vantage points. Its natural beauty always captivated her.

"Spectacular, isn't it?" Brandon questioned, coming

up softly behind her as though he felt his footsteps might intrude on her appreciation of the magnificent vista. She heard the roughness in his voice again. And all at once she realized that the compelling natural scene had touched his feelings, too.

"So you did mean it—about this being what sold you on living here?" she murmured.

"Yes. I liked the house, even though it was a bit larger than what I was looking for. But when I stepped out on the deck and saw this . . ."

For more than a minute neither of them spoke. Somehow the clear air, the tall pines and the silvery rapids far below had created a bridge between herself and Brandon, a bridge that Laura really didn't want to cross.

Taking a few steps farther along the railing, she cleared her throat. "You're right, this scenery deserves a lot more expansive viewing area," she agreed, making an effort to shake off the intimacy of the moment.

"Tell me what you'd like to put here," Brandon urged, wishing that she weren't pulling back from him again. His hand reached out to touch her shoulder and then reluctantly stopped before actually making the contact.

"You want a much broader, more dramatic deck with several levels," Laura began, back in her professional role once more. "I'd suggest wrapping it around the side of the house—and joining it to the front of the property with a flight of steps."

"So no one else plays Jack and Jill and comes tumbling down the hill?"

Laura couldn't hold back a grin. "You've got to admit that would be safer."

"Would the deck be able to support a hot tub?" he asked.

"Only if there's a lot of reinforcement from the bottom."

They went back inside and sat down at the card table to discuss Laura's landscaping ideas. "I'll make some sketches and get back to you," she finished, picking up her note pad.

"But how do you know your plans are going to really fit my needs?" Brandon questioned, pushing back his chair and standing up.

"What do you mean?"

"Don't you usually take a client's lifestyle into consideration when you draw up your designs?"

Laura nodded.

"Well, you don't know anything about my lifestyle," Brandon pointed out, standing up and walking to the window. "In fact, you know hardly anything about me. Suppose I had a . . ." He hesitated for a moment and then plowed ahead. "A wife and children joining me next month. Wouldn't you design a different sort of deck than if I told you I was a swinging bachelor who likes to throw big outdoor parties?"

"Do you have a wife and children?" Laura found herself asking.

He turned quickly to meet her eyes. "No."

She hadn't realized she'd been holding her breath, waiting for the answer.

"And I don't like to throw large parties, either," he added. "But there's bound to be a lot more you should know to do your job properly. So I suggest that you stay and have dinner so we can get to know each other a little better."

Laura pushed back her chair and stood up. "I'm afraid I hadn't planned on anything like that," she began.

"But there's no one you have to fix dinner for, is there?"

"No."

"Then why not come on in the kitchen and give me a hand."

As he spoke, Brandon crossed the room and disappeared through a door at the other end of the dining ell. It was obvious that he expected her to follow. From the next room she could hear the sound of running water.

She supposed he was washing the last of the mulch off his hands.

"Do you like teriyaki steak?" he called. "With stir-fried vegetables and rice?"

Laura stuck her head around the corner to see him turning two thick pieces of beef marinating in a glass dish.

"When did you start those?" she asked.

"Right after I left the garden center."

"You were certainly taking a chance on wasting a lot of good meat."

"I could have saved half of it for tomorrow. Come on in and help me cut up some vegetables."

She had fully intended to leave after their consultation. Now, almost in spite of herself, Laura stepped across the threshold, noting that the large country kitchen looked a lot more lived in than the rest of the house. Stainless-steel pots hung from a black metal rack in the center of the work area, glass canisters of grains and legumes lined one side of the counter, and a wooden chopping block and knife waited near the sink.

"This does give me some idea of your priorities," she noted, looking with interest at the shelves of the well-stocked pantry.

"Yup," Brandon acknowledged, pouring rice into a saucepan on the stove. "I figured I could always sleep on the floor, but I hate to eat in restaurants on a regular basis. Say, maybe you should add a gas barbecue grill to the deck."

"I'll make a note of that."

"Make it a mental note. And while you're doing that, why don't you see what vegetables you'd like. They're in the crisper."

"Do you always just assume people are going to go along with your whims?" Laura questioned as she washed up at the sink.

"Asking you to stay to dinner wasn't a whim." The words brought that familiar husky quality to his voice.

"Oh." Laura turned quickly to the refrigerator and

opened the door with a hand that trembled slightly. She knelt down automatically to inspect the contents of the crisper. But as she did, she had the feeling that maybe it would be best to stand up and leave before she got any more involved with Brandon McGuire. Nonetheless, she knew it wasn't what she was going to do. She did want to get to know this man better. She was curious about where he had come from and what he was doing in Harperstown, and—if the truth be known—whether he really was sleeping on the floor.

Lost in thought, she pulled out broccoli, scallions, Chinese cabbage and green pepper.

"I should have asked before I pressed you into service, but do you like to cook?" her host asked as she washed the vegetables.

"Yes. I learned when I was still in junior high. Mom worked late at the garden center two or three nights a week, and she'd leave me directions for fixing dinner."

"Did the garden center belong to your parents, then?"

"Yes. I took over when Dad had to retire because of his asthma and high blood pressure. They're in New Mexico now."

"I've heard the air out there is marvelous. Did his health improve?"

"Yes. Thank goodness."

It was easy to talk to this man, Laura reflected as she began to chop the cabbage. In fact, he was somehow effortlessly establishing a comfortable familiarity between them that she knew would have been impossible with someone else.

What's more, they had fallen into a smooth working rhythm. While she took care of the vegetables, he heated up the broiler and tended the rice.

"When did you learn to cook?" she asked.

"In college. The dining hall food was so bad that I moved out of the dorm and took an apartment with two other students who were also starving to death. Luckily one of us already knew a carrot scraper from a spatula or we would have had to rely on TV dinners."

Laura laughed. And then she glanced over speculatively at Brandon. "I didn't know many guys in college who could cook."

"Neither did I."

"So just who was that talented roommate of yours?"

"Margie O'Connor. Say, you're an expert vegetable cutter," he complimented. "What's your culinary specialty?"

"You're changing the subject."

"You noticed. How do you like your steak, by the way?"

"Medium."

"Me too. Actually, I wonder how the 'rare is best' mystique got started."

"You didn't tell me what you specialize in," Brandon pointed out as he bent down to take the wok from a lower cabinet.

Laura thought for a moment. "I like oriental cooking too. Kung Po chicken is one of my favorites."

"So you're the hot and spicy type. Maybe I should have put some red peppers in the marinade."

Laura shot him a disbelieving glance. There was no good way to respond to that comment, so she simply kept working in silence.

When the food was done, they filled their plates in the kitchen and carried them out to the card table. Brandon produced a bottle of Burgundy and two water glasses.

"Sorry," he apologized as he poured them each some of the wine. "But I haven't had much time for shopping."

"So what are you doing here in Harperstown?" Laura asked, cutting a piece of steak.

"My company, General Development Corporation, is going to locate an executive conference center in the middle of downtown—if we get the zoning change we need, that is."

Laura's eyes widened. "So you're the one who was buying up all those antebellum townhouses."

Brandon nodded.

"You know, there was a lot of speculation about who was scarfing up all that property—and for what. One rumor had the federal government clearing the area for a low-income housing project. Another claimed a group of investors was looking for a site for an experimental urban solid waste disposal plant. And I swear"—Laura paused and held up her hand palm outward—"some people were whispering that it was a mob take-over."

Brandon threw back his head and laughed. "Well, don't start calling me Godfather. We don't have anything to do with the underworld."

Laura rolled her eyes. "I didn't subscribe to the mob theory. But I am curious about all the secrecy."

"Believe me, it was necessary. Once people know a parcel of land is valuable, the price goes up—a lot."

Laura nodded. "I guess that makes sense."

"Actually," Brandon continued, "a mortgage banking firm handled the purchases. They were able to acquire the properties at quite a competitive price."

"There are a lot of people in town who don't want to see that property pass out of local control—or be torn down, either. You may be in for quite a fight, you know." With a few carefully chosen words, she filled him in on some of the intricacies of local politics.

Brandon set down his fork. "Thanks for the insights. But I'm hoping that when I present our proposal to the zoning board, the opposition will evaporate. I'm not out to destroy Harperstown's historic charm. That's one of the things that attracted us in the first place. We're planning to incorporate many of the existing structures into the conference center complex—along with a mid-rise that will blend in with the surrounding property."

For the next few minutes, Brandon elaborated on the plans, and Laura could see how excited he was about the endeavor.

"If preparation counts for anything, you should do all right. How many projects like this have you set up?"

"This is my first. Before this I was more involved in other aspects of the business. But I spent the last year at Cornell getting my master's in hotel management so I'd know what I was doing. You don't know what it's like taking on an intensive course load like that after you've been out of school for ten years."

Laura nodded. "So why did you do it?"

"I wanted to try something new." The way he clipped out the statement was designed to warn her away from further questions in that direction. And Laura got the message. After all, wasn't she herself a specialist in that particular technique for cutting off discussion?

For a moment neither of them seemed to know what to say. Then Brandon pushed back his chair. "Can I get you anything else?"

"No thanks. That was delicious. But I really didn't mean to stay this late." While they had been eating, the sun had disappeared. Now the almost empty house was dark and shadowy except for the pools of illumination cast by the few overhead lights. Suddenly Laura was very aware that she hadn't intended to stay for dinner in the first place. She picked up her plate and carried it quickly to the kitchen.

"Just leave that on the counter," he called after her. "I'll get them later. How about some coffee? I found a store in town where you can buy beans for grinding."

"No thanks," she repeated. "I really should be getting back. I'll call you in a day or two, and we can make an appointment to look at my sketches." Her voice conveyed its own message—that she was trying once again to put this professional consultation on the impersonal level where it had never really been. Returning to the dining room, she reached for her note pad. Before she could pick it up, Brandon was out of his seat.

He knew that his own abrupt manner a moment ago had given her the impetus to distance herself from him again. Yet her innocent question had caught him off-balance, and his old, self-protective habits had simply taken over.

But now that he had gotten to know Laura Carson better, he didn't want their dinner together to end this way. He hadn't felt so happy and relaxed in years as he had with her this evening. And somehow, despite her naturally warm personality, he suspected that letting go and just enjoying a man's company was a rare event for her as well.

"Don't leave yet," he said simply.

But she shook her head. It had been a mistake to stay for dinner and give him a chance to get around her defenses. For she knew instinctively that was what he had been doing.

He searched her face, seeing that her eyes had become like opaque glass, giving nothing away.

He wanted to reach her again, to communicate with the easy intimacy they had established during the meal. But that was no longer possible. The lines of verbal exchange had been cut as effectively as though someone had severed a telephone cord.

A thought flashed through his mind: Was it possible to meet a woman and know almost immediately that there was going to be something very special between the two of you? Yesterday he would have scoffed at the idea. But that was before he had encountered Laura.

He knew she felt it too—perhaps more vividly than he did. And yet, for her own private reasons, she was fighting it for all she was worth.

There was more he could have said. But it would have been wasted breath. Instead, he took her by the shoulders, his fingers instantly conscious of her satiny flesh beneath the soft fabric of her flannel shirt. For a moment the intensity of his gaze captured hers.

This was communication on a very basic level. There was no way Laura could deny the purpose in the heated depths of his dark eyes. He was going to kiss her.

She felt his hands slide around to her back and watched mesmerized as his lips descended to meet hers. Her awareness of him was something she knew she should fight. But that was impossible, she acknowledged with a little tremor. His closeness was too overwhelming, his hands too insistent as they moved against her shoulder blades, the male aroma of his body too enticing. She felt his warm breath first as the lightest of caresses. Then his lips were covering hers in a kiss that was at once gentle and demanding, urgent and seductive.

This moment had been inevitable between them, she realized now. She had known it and been afraid of it almost from the first.

As Brandon's lips moved against hers, she felt an unaccustomed warmth spreading through her body. Suddenly it was hard to stand without clinging to his hard frame, as she had clung earlier that afternoon. Then she had been shaken by her headlong slide down the hill. Now she was shaken by a force she barely understood and yet could not deny.

Brandon felt the response, felt her arms steal around his neck and her body mold itself to his like honey clinging to a spoon. He deepened the kiss, his tongue breaching the barrier of her teeth to investigate the velvety territory beyond.

He felt her deep sigh of pleasure against his mouth. And it was all he could do to keep from trailing his hands down her back to cup her rounded little bottom and pull her even more firmly against himself. It was what he had been thinking about when he brushed that mulch off the seat of her jeans. Hell, it was what he had been thinking about all afternoon. But he hadn't really intended to kiss her—not tonight, at any rate.

The way she trembled in his arms, however, and the way her lips had begun to move so enticingly under his were assurances that, at least for now, it had been the right thing to do. It was impossible not to give in to the exquisite satisfaction of the moment. He had known it would be like this between them. He had known that the intensity of her response would match his own. And he couldn't stop himself from increasing the intimacy of the kiss, from plundering all the sweetness of her mouth with his lips and tongue.

He wanted to keep on holding her like this, kissing her like this. He ached to shift her body so that he could cup the tantalizing fullness of her breasts. But he didn't dare go that far with her—not this time.

"Laura," he murmured, shifting her body now so that he could put a few inches between them. "Laura."

The sound of her name made her eyes fly open. Suddenly she was hit with the reality of just how tightly she had been clinging to Brandon and how her mouth had melded itself with his. Almost as an act of self-defense, her hands came up to push against his chest.

What had come over her? she wondered, not sure how things had progressed so far so quickly. But there was one thing she did know. She had to get away, to put some distance between herself and Brandon McGuire before anything more could happen.

"Please . . ." she began.

His hands dropped to his sides. "Yes. I know." He wanted to say more, to say everything. Yet he knew that if he tried to hold her now, it would only make things worse. And so he simply took a step back.

Whirling, she fled the room, fled the house, hurrying to the safety of her car. But she knew there was really no place she could hide from the feelings this man had kindled within her.

3

Afterward Laura didn't remember climbing into her Datsun and starting the engine. When she finally refocused on her surroundings, she was turning in at the long gravel drive of the farmhouse where she had lived since she was a girl.

She had told herself she was fleeing Brandon McGuire and the feelings he had aroused when he pulled her into his arms and kissed her. But, just as surely, she was trying to outdistance her own memories.

After turning off the engine, Laura squeezed her eyes shut and clenched her fists until her nails dug into the tender flesh of her palms. But it was impossible to stop a series of vivid pictures from flashing across the screen of her mind like scenes from the coming attractions at the movies. Though these particular images recorded the past, it was hard not to think of them as harbingers—of what would happen again if she let another man breach the barriers she had so painstakingly erected.

Could it only be seven years? It might have been a lifetime ago that she had so joyfully agreed to marry Arthur Henderson. They had met on a ski trip when she was a sophomore in college and he was in his second year of law school. He had asked her to marry him after they'd dated for only a few months. And she had thought he loved her enough to accept her as she was. But there was one important fact she knew she must confide before their marriage—that she would probably never be able to have children.

That Sunday night, Arthur seemed to take the news in stride. He had kissed her as usual before returning to school in Baltimore, where his family had lived for generations. So she hadn't been prepared for the letter that arrived a few days later, telling her how sorry he was to have to break their engagement. He was sure she'd understand his position, but his parents expected him to carry on the family line. If he'd only known the facts about Laura before, things never would have gone so far.

Now she pressed her palms against her eyelids, trying to blot out the remembered black letters against the white sheet of paper. Arthur had implied that she'd deceived him. But just when did you inform a man that you were barren? she asked herself with a hollow little laugh. Did you introduce the subject when he asked you for a first date? "Say, by the way, I think I'd better tell you before we go out that I can't have any children—just in case your feelings for me might incline toward marriage, that is."

The idea was ludicrous. But what was the answer? Did you keep silent and let things progress as they had with Arthur? Or did you make it clear you only wanted to have an affair?

Laura shook her head sadly. The idea of a casual sexual relationship went against her ingrained sense of morality. On the other hand, she couldn't risk a rejection like Arthur's again, either. Long ago she had concluded that it was much safer to keep her dealings with men impersonal, to rely on her work for her joys and her satisfactions.

It had been relatively easy to stick to that logical decision—until Brandon McGuire had pulled her into his arms and devastated her with his kiss.

The shadows under Laura's eyes the next morning testified to her sleepless night. Thoughts of the past, and of Brandon, had chased themselves around her restless mind until she'd finally fallen asleep a few hours before the alarm was scheduled to go off.

As she forced herself to get out of bed, her glance fell on the note pad she had tossed onto her chair. A small shred of mulch clung to the spiral binding. Laura stared at it for a second. Then, reaching out with forefinger and thumb, she pulled it free and set it carefully on her dresser. The gesture triggered a decision. It would be easy to avoid Brandon McGuire by turning down his job. But landscaping his lot and following through with the construction work he wanted was just too good an opportunity to pass up, she told herself.

The rational part of her mind had a perfectly logical argument for the decision. Since taking over Carson's, Laura had thrived on challenges. And she certainly wasn't going to walk away from one now. If the man represented a threat to her equanimity, so be it. Actually, she should be grateful that Brandon McGuire was giving her the opportunity to prove something important—to both of them. She had her own life firmly in control. And the next time they met, she would let him know in no uncertain terms that there was going to be nothing else personal between them.

Forty minutes later, as she pushed open the door of the garden center, she felt more like her usual chipper self. A hot shower had helped to soothe her tension. And a bit of makeup had camouflaged the circles under her eyes.

"Well, you look like you're ready to grab a tiger by the

tail this morning," Sylvia Gordon commented as she spied the determined set of Laura's delicately molded jaw.

An energetic widow in her late fifties, Sylvia was not only Carson's second-in-command, but an old friend of the family. She had started working at the garden center when her husband died ten years before. And she'd taken much of the load from the senior Carsons' shoulders while Laura was finishing up her master's degree. She still handled many of the day-to-day details of the operation, freeing Laura to spend much of her time on design and construction supervision.

Her employer grinned. "I'm not after any tigers, just a landscape and construction job that's going to be a real bear. It's for that new house on Littlefield Road—the one that's practically hanging out over the valley."

"I guess that means you're going to be holed up in your office all morning with a note pad and graph paper," Sylvia observed. "So before you disappear, could you okay these work schedules?"

Laura picked up the forms and gave them a quick once-over. "Sylvia, you know I have complete trust in your decisions," she pointed out. "If I went to the seashore for a month, I'd come back knowing you and the rest of the staff had everything running smoothly."

"Oh, go on," Sylvia protested. But she couldn't hold back a pleased smile.

Laura stayed to chat for a few minutes and discuss some other business details.

"I'll handle all the calls—unless something really needs your attention," Sylvia called out just before the younger woman shut the door to her office.

Opening her briefcase, Laura pulled out the preliminary sketch she had made at Brandon's house the afternoon before. She should have gotten the back and side elevations, too. But somehow, after her slide down the hill, that had completely slipped her mind.

However, her memory for detail had been honed by

years of practice. When she closed her eyes, she could recall the other views almost perfectly.

Once she started to work, her pencil fairly flew over the page, sketching in the wide multilevel deck she had envisioned, the dramatically landscaped entranceway, the side terracing, and the steps that would connect the front and back of the property. The plantings would blend in with the woodsy setting, and the decking would be cantilevered out over the valley to give Brandon a sense of connection with the natural scene. The hot tub he had requested would be tucked into the corner of the deck farthest from the stairs. The barbecue would flank the sliding glass doors.

Leaning back in her chair, Laura flipped through the sketches again. Sometimes it took days to come up with a completely unified concept like this. Often she wasn't satisfied with her first ideas—or her second, or her third. That was not the case this morning. She liked what she saw very much.

But then, she knew why. This wasn't just a set of abstract designs. They were for a particular person. And he had been right. Because she had taken the time to get to know him better the night before, she had produced concepts that fit the ideas she had formed of the man.

Would Brandon understand that? she wondered, closing the note pad and smoothing her hand across the cover. Would he like the work as much as she did? Would he know how much of *herself* she had revealed in these drawings?

Putting down her pencil, she sighed. Why did she have to be drawn to this particular man, she wondered, when it had been so easy to keep others at arm's length?

She didn't know the answer. But she did know that the magnetic pull had started with their first contact, with his voice. The attraction had only grown stronger when they had actually met.

It wasn't just Brandon's considerable physical presence, however. It was the sensitivity under his very male exterior, his enthusiasm for his job, his unselfconscious sense of humor. He had even laughed at himself, she remembered. That had been the first step in disarming her yesterday.

But there was something else, too. Something she could not yet admit. Even when he had been casual and joking, Brandon had made her feel *wanted*. It had been a warm current flowing from him. And, like a hibernating animal burrowed into the cold earth, she had awakened to his renewing warmth and even basked in it.

For a long time Laura sat staring into space. Usually she was in firm control of herself. She was able to make decisions quickly and stick to them. But not this time. One moment she had absolutely decided to put an end to her budding relationship with Brandon. The next moment, she wondered if she could.

As if to emphasize her ambivalence, one of the lighted buttons on Laura's phone began to blink. Whom had Sylvia decided to put through? she wondered, reaching out to pick up the receiver.

"Laura?" The familiar mellow timbre of Brandon's voice brought back immediate memories of their first contact—and of their last.

"Yes."

"Who is that dragon you have guarding your phone line? I thought I wasn't going to get to talk to you."

"Dragon?" Laura was incredulous. "You can't mean Sylvia. She's a gray-haired grandmother—in tennis shoes."

"Then you must have put her through a formidable basic training course." There was a note of amusement in his voice now.

"She was just standing sentry at the castle gate so I could work on your sketches."

"Oh. So you've been locked away in your ivory tower. Are you finished with the sketches? I'm anxious to see what you've got for me."

Laura took the receiver away from her face and stared

at it for a moment. "You know," she began, "sometimes it takes me weeks to come up with a design that I feel really does justice to the house and terrain I'm working with."

"But in this case . . ." Brandon prompted.

Laura gave up. "All right. In this case, I do have some designs that I think you'll like," she admitted, unable to keep a note of pride out of her voice. Now why had she gone and bragged about that?

As she had somehow known he would, Brandon turned her words to his own advantage. "Great. Then I'll be by the office to have a look at them this afternoon. See you later."

Without giving her a chance to demur, he ended the conversation.

Laura sighed and put down the receiver. Brandon McGuire had just gotten his way by moving quickly and decisively again. She should feel annoyed with herself—and with him, too. Instead she felt a mixture of eagerness and trepidation stirring inside her.

Pushing back her chair, she stood up and crossed to the window where she adjusted the slats of the mini-blinds so that she could look out once again on the well-laid-out gardens that surrounded Carson's converted barn. They had been one of her first projects when she was still in graduate school. And she was pleased with how well they had turned out. Often, while she thought about a problem or planned a design, she liked to let her gaze wander up and down the winding brick paths. Usually the exercise was calming. But not this morning.

What was she planning to do, she wondered, stand around like a wooden Indian and simply wait for Mr. McGuire to show up?

Recrossing her office, she pulled open the door and strode out into the showroom. If Gary hadn't finished unloading yesterday's shipment from the depot, maybe she could help.

But before she reached the service area in the back, Sylvia flagged her down. "I hope you didn't mind my putting that call through."

"Oh, no," Laura assured her. "I was finished with what I was doing, anyway."

Sylvia waited for a moment as though expecting some further information about the caller. But Laura failed to volunteer anything more.

"Well," the older woman went on, glancing at her watch, "I was beginning to wonder if you were going to take a lunch break today. Want me to send for some sandwiches from Tony's?" The little family-run deli down the road was one of the few places nearby where they could get a meal. Luckily the food was excellent.

"No, I'll go get them," Laura volunteered. "I could use some exercise after sitting at my desk all morning. What do you want?"

Twenty minutes later, after her short hike, Laura felt more relaxed. The nippy air had made her walk quickly. And she was also gleefully anticipating Sylvia's reaction to the dessert she'd brought back.

"Now listen," she began, as she set out the food on the picnic table in the workroom, "don't get angry, but Tony made one of his cherry cheesecakes this morning. If you'd seen it, you'd understand why I brought back a piece for us to split."

"Laura! You didn't!"

"A half a piece isn't going to break either one of us."

Sylvia rolled her eyes. "All right. Since you've brought it back, I guess I won't refuse."

"That's what I was counting on," Laura responded, unwrapping a tuna sandwich.

Sylvia set down two cups of tea and pulled up the bench opposite her employer.

"Okay," she began, "I've been waiting patiently for almost an hour. But you haven't said a word about him. Just who exactly is Brandon McGuire?"

Laura almost choked on the bite she'd just taken.

"What do you mean, who is Brandon McGuire?" she countered. "Don't tell me you've met him?"

"Just over the phone. That man has got the sexiest voice I've ever heard—and the most persistence," she added. "I told him I wasn't going to interrupt you. But he wouldn't take no for an answer."

"That's him all right," Laura agreed before biting into her sandwich and very deliberately beginning to chew.

"So you're not going to talk with your mouth full," Sylvia observed. "But I can wait."

Laura looked at her friend and employee. "He's just a man who's moved to town and wants us to landscape his lot and build a deck on the outside of his house."

"If you say so. But I'd be willing to bet that talking to you was the most important thing he had to do this morning."

Laura could think of no reply. To cover the gap in the conversation, she took several sips of tea. "What kind of response have we gotten to that ad for spring and summer help?" she finally asked.

Sylvia shot her a perceptive look. But it was clear she realized the previous subject was closed. As they shared the cherry cheesecake, they discussed business matters.

"You're right; it was good," Sylvia conceded, forking up the last of her half.

"What's life without its small pleasures?" Laura countered.

Sylvia seemed about to say something and then thought better of it. "Right," she agreed, and then turned to clear the picnic table.

Laura glanced at the window. "Now that the sun's out again, I think I'll have a look around the grounds," she murmured as she opened the workroom door.

Once outside, she headed for the beds of purple and white crocuses planted along one side of the converted barn. There was something about this time of year that always exhilarated her. Later in the season the gardens around Carson's might offer a riot of bright colors. But early spring brought Laura a sense of keen anticipation as she looked for the emerging green plants that signaled the renewal of life.

She was kneeling down, counting tender green shoots, when she heard a sound behind her on the brick path and whirled around to find her eyes level with a pair of jeans-clad thighs.

"How long have you been standing there?" Laura inquired.

"Not very. You know, when the sun glints on your hair, it brings out red highlights I never noticed before," Brandon mused.

"Does it?"

"Yes." Taking her by the elbows, he helped her to her feet, but he didn't immediately let go. For a moment they stood very close, facing each other. She felt his gaze as though it were a caress. Yet when he spoke again, his words were light and totally unexpected.

"Cherry candy?" he asked.

"What?"

"Have you been eating cherry candy?" he repeated.

"No. Cherry cheesecake. Sylvia and I shared a piece," she added irrelevantly.

He leaned closer, his eyes on her slightly parted lips. "I wish it had been with me."

Flustered, Laura took a step backwards. How did this man manage to turn even a simple conversation into an intimate encounter? she wondered. This was just a business call, and she was going to keep it that way. "You'll want to see those designs." As she spoke, she was already walking rapidly back toward the garden center.

Sylvia looked up from her paper work as they came in the door. When she saw Brandon, she raised a questioning eyebrow, but Laura didn't pause to relieve the other woman's curiosity as she headed back toward her office. Brandon, however, turned and grinned at the gray-haired woman before lengthening his stride in order to catch up with Laura. Following her into the office, he shut the door.

"The sketches are right here," she announced in her most no-nonsense voice, opening a manila folder and handing the contents across her desk. Wordlessly, Brandon accepted the sheets and then sat down in the chair opposite.

She watched as he shuffled rapidly through the pile and then took the time to look at each drawing more thoroughly. For several minutes he said nothing. And Laura found herself watching his face. She knew this was some of her best work. Most clients would have made some complimentary remarks as they looked over the sketches. But Brandon made no comment at all.

When he finally looked up, their eyes met. "These are absolutely marvelous, Laura. You've captured exactly the feeling I was hoping for with the landscaping. And the deck is really magnificent."

"I—I'm glad you're pleased," she acknowledged, knowing that she wasn't just mumbling a polite rejoinder.

"So when can you start the actual work?"

"Not immediately. There are several jobs ahead of yours, and at this time of year, we only have a small crew working." As she spoke, she got up and crossed to the window, falling back on the old habit of looking out over her domain while she considered the scheduling. "I think we'll be able to start the last week in March, weather permitting."

"I'm disappointed that you can't make it sooner," Brandon replied, getting up and walking to stand in back of her.

Although he didn't touch her, she could feel his very male presence directly behind her. In response, the back of her neck prickled.

For several heartbeats, neither of them spoke. And then she heard Brandon clear his throat.

"Laura, there's something we have to talk about." He

might have been referring to the work schedule, but the hard edge in his voice told her that wasn't the case.

She felt her hands automatically ball themselves into small fists. If she could have taken a step forward to put some more distance between them, she would have done so. But she wasn't an escape artist. She couldn't walk through the window sash. If she turned around, she would be face-to-face with him, as close as they had been outside in the garden. Almost as close as they had been last night when he'd kissed her. And she didn't want that. She had told herself she could handle Brandon when they met again. But that had been a pipe dream.

"Please leave," she whispered.

"No."

She sensed exasperation, determination, domination in that one syllable. As if to emphasize the point, he reached out and wrapped his hands around her fists. A moment ago his very presence had held her captive. Now she might have been bound to him by steel chains.

"We have to talk," he repeated, pulling her gently backwards so that her body rested lightly yet firmly against his.

As her back touched his broad chest, she was unable to suppress a shiver—part fear, part sexual awareness. There was no way, she knew, that Brandon could not have felt her reaction.

"No, we don't have anything to talk about," she denied, trying as well to deny the steel bonds and pull herself away. But it took the merest effort on his part to keep her where he wanted her.

"I'm going to speak my piece now, whether you want to listen or not," his voice rumbled from behind her, rough with an emotion that might have been anger—or something else just as basic.

With her back pressed against the front of his body, it was impossible for him not to remember how she had trembled in his arms the night before. She had responded to him as dry kindling to a match. Yet he knew that desire hadn't been her only emotion.

"Laura, you're afraid of what happened between us, of what's *going* to happen between us, aren't you?"

Her answer was a muffled sound that she wished had not escaped her throat.

But Brandon gave no quarter. "Laura, there's got to be a good reason why a woman responds to a man the way you did to me last night and then turns and runs away from him. I'm not going to ask what it is. But it's impossible for me not to speculate, to make assumptions."

She didn't want to hear his guesses about what was wrong with her. Desperately, she tried to pull away again. It was wasted effort.

"I won't let you go this time until I'm finished," Brandon warned.

"Then hurry up and finish," she flung over her shoulder. But she couldn't keep her voice from quavering.

"Stop fighting me, Laura. And I don't mean just physically. I'm not going to ask you to tell me about whatever it is that's made you afraid of intimacy," Brandon continued. "In fact, I don't *want* you to tell me. I know you're not ready for that yet."

Laura bit her lip, wishing that he would simply turn her loose and leave.

"I understand that this is painful for you," he acknowledged, as though speaking her thoughts aloud. "But if I leave now, you're going to build up a wall between us so thick that I may not be able to break through. And I can't let that happen."

She held herself completely still, making no reply.

"Are you listening to me?" he demanded, his hands tightening over hers. He was unable to keep himself from giving her body a slight shake.

"Yes," she managed.

As though he realized he was pushing too hard, his manner seemed to soften. "Laura, maybe I'd better come right out and say what I've wanted to say since last night. Give me a chance, will you? Give *us* a chance. Don't assume that I'm someone I'm not."

Had she heard him right? she wondered. She had met this man yesterday, and here he was laying some sort of claim to her. Yet she had felt the intensity of whatever it was between them right from the first, just as he had. That was part of what had sparked her fear.

He paused for a moment and moved his head so that his cheek caressed the top of her hair. "I'm not going to push you," he whispered. "I know how you feel. I've been hurt, too—badly enough so that I'm still cautious. I'm not ready to talk about what happened to me either. But neither one of us has to do that—until we get to know each other better. All I'm asking for is the chance to do that."

She had been resisting his onslaught with all the strength she possessed. But those last words were her undoing. He wasn't negotiating from a position of power after all. He was letting her see his own vulnerability. The realization opened a wellspring of feelings, of mingled fear and hope.

"Brandon, I want to trust you," she began. "But it's been such a long time since . . ." She couldn't finish the sentence, so she began again in a voice that was almost a whisper. "All I can do is tell you I'll try."

He knew what a giant step it was for her to speak those words.

"That's all I need to know for now," he reassured her. "That you won't simply shut me out."

She hadn't realized she was trembling until he let go of her balled fists to lightly stroke her arms. Then his hands went up to touch the sides of her face. They moved inward to trace the lines of her eyebrows, the plane of her nose, the outline of her lips. As Laura relaxed against his tense frame, she heard him sigh.

His hands continued to gentle her, caressing her face and neck before pushing aside the dark curtain of her hair to find her ear. His fingertips were warm on her skin. They told her what she had been afraid to acknowledge before—that he wanted her, and not just sexually.

It had been eons since she had felt such warmth and caring from another human being. And it was impossible not to respond. Had she really denied herself this kind of closeness for so long? Laura wondered, amazed now at her own stoicism.

"Laura," he murmured, his voice like dark velvet now as he sensed the extent of her surrender. "When I found you in the garden, you were looking at the new shoots coming up out of the ground. You know, they don't have to worry about what they're doing. They just react automatically to the sun warming the cold earth." As he spoke, his fingers moved down her neck to her shoulders and then to her sides, sliding up and down her ribs, sending sensual messages through her body.

"But it's not that simple for people, is it?" he continued. "We have to think, analyze, examine motives. How much easier it would be if we could simply trust ourselves to respond to our feelings."

"It's not just trusting ourselves," she whispered. "It's trusting other people."

"I know. And I'll give you the time for that. I promise."

For a moment they stood there together without speaking. Then, ever so lightly, his hands inched inward, finding and caressing the sides of her breasts with long, silky strokes that made her close her eyes tightly and lean back against him.

She felt her nipples tighten in anticipation of his touch. She felt her neck arch and her lips part. She knew that if they had been facing each other, her mouth would have instinctively sought his. But Brandon made no move to turn her around.

"I'm not going to push you," he repeated, his breath warming her ear.

He held her for another moment. And then, gently, he released her and took a half step backwards.

"But I'd better beat a hasty retreat before I break my promise," he added huskily.

4

Laura was humming the melody of a popular tune as she got ready for a date with Brandon one Friday evening a couple of weeks later. She'd spent time with him almost every day, and she was surprised and pleased at her increasing ability to simply relax and enjoy their relationship.

As she adjusted the water for her shower, she had to admit that she felt happier and more carefree than she had in a long time. It was almost as if she had been taking a daily dose of tranquilizers for the last few years and had suddenly stopped, she mused, stepping under the hot spray and feeling the water tingle against her skin.

Since Brandon had persuaded her to let him into her life, everything seemed different. Colors were more vivid. Tastes more sweet or pungent. The first flowers of spring more tenderly fragile in their transitory beauty. It was as though every day were a present to be unwrapped and savored—and, most of all, shared.

The afternoon Brandon had come to her office to look

at the sketches, he had reached her on a very fundamental level. But once having forced his way past her defensive barriers, he had kept his initial promise. He hadn't pushed her into anything she couldn't handle. Instead, they had simply enjoyed each other's company and gotten to know each other better.

One thing that surprised Laura was how much delight she took in rediscovering the attractions of the Harperstown area with a newcomer. About a week after she'd finished the plans for the deck, she and Brandon drove down to the site where his company hoped to locate its executive conference center. Laura didn't often go to the center of town, so it was easy to look at things as though she were actually seeing them for the first time.

Over the past few years the population of the area had grown to almost 120,000. The greatest part of that development was outside the city limits, so many of the buildings downtown were old and in disrepair. But here and there, areas had been fixed up to make charming little enclaves of shops with antebellum character. Laura could understand why Brandon had seen the area's potential.

The block his company had chosen was a bit too far west to be fashionable. But it was close enough to the main business district.

As they got out of the Blazer, she paused for a moment, looking with interest at the old townhouses his company had purchased.

"Most of the structures are basically sound. The major problem will be to refurbish the interiors—after we put in new plumbing and wiring, that is."

He pointed down a narrow alley. "See that group of buildings? They're the only ones that are going to have to come down. But I think the mid-rise we've designed to replace them will be completely compatible with the area."

Laura nodded. She had secretly wondered whether a project like this could work. Now her artist's imagination could see how the charming details of these antique facades would look with clean brick and new paint. "Coming to a conference here will be a lot different from staying in an ordinary hotel," she mused. "I suppose you're going to use a colonial motif in the bedrooms?"

"That's right. And we'll use the new building for the lobby, conference rooms and dining facilities. I'd take you around back," he added, "but this particular alley isn't exactly the show spot of Harperstown."

"I've heard. If all you do is haul away the trash that's collected back there, you'll be doing something important for the city."

"Oh, I intend to do more than clean out the old tires and discarded washing machines," Brandon went on, warming to the subject. "The interior of the block is going to feature a multileveled landscaped courtyard. Want to design it?"

"What a question! That would be fantastic. I've been telling the businessmen around here for years that the downtown area needed some focus like that. But nobody would listen."

"Well, you've got my ear—and anything else you want," Brandon chuckled. "As soon as the architectural plans for the complex arrive, I'll let you have a look so you can start integrating your own ideas."

The next day was unusually warm for the end of March. In exchange for Brandon's tour of the conference center site, Laura suggested that they play hooky from work and visit the undeveloped part of the river valley near his house.

"I'll make a picnic lunch," she offered.

"Only if you let me do my share and bring the dessert."

It was not quite noon when they pulled the Blazer onto the gravel shoulder of the road high above the valley.

"Are you sure we can make it down there?" Brandon asked, eyeing the rocky, twisting path that led down toward the river. "The last time you did some climbing around, as I recall, you ended up on your bottom in the mulch."

Laura finished adjusting her backpack and turned to him with an exaggerated scowl. "This is entirely different. I've been climbing around here since I was a kid."

"You mean you used to be a surefooted little mountain goat?" he asked innocently.

"No. But I'm beginning to suspect that you're a chicken."

Instead of dignifying her retort with an answer, Brandon simply started down the trail.

As it turned out, the descent wasn't as difficult as it looked. And when they finally stopped to rest on a wide rock hanging out over a small waterfall, Brandon turned to her with a warm smile. "You're right," he agreed, pitching his voice to carry over the sound of the cascading water. "The trek down was worth it. It's hard to believe the city is less than ten miles away." As he spoke he looked around at the soft moss and grasses that lined the riverbanks, and at the towering gray rock that guarded the canyon walls.

Laura nodded. "I know. When my friends and I came here, we used to pretend we were pioneers like Daniel Boone or explorers facing an uncharted wilderness. I think I spent some of the happiest Saturdays of my childhood sloshing along this river valley."

Putting an arm over her shoulder, Brandon pulled her closer and she nestled comfortably against him. She had sensed that he would like this place as much as she. For a few moments they simply listened to the cadence of the falling water and watched a cautious blue jay inspect them from a tree limb across the river. Then Brandon shifted her in his arms so that they were facing each other. She looked up into his dark eyes, seeing her own contentment mirrored there. Her lips curved into a smile, and he reached out with the tip of his finger to trace the upturned curve.

"I'm glad you brought me here." Even above the natural music of the cataract, she could sense the husky vibrations in his voice.

He bent to kiss her then. Their kiss began with that sweet anticipation she had so quickly come to expect, and then deepened into a warm mingling of sensations and emotions—emotions she still could not express in words.

"That wasn't lunch, was it?" Brandon questioned. His tone was light, and yet below the surface she could sense the power of needs and desires held in check.

"No," she answered, striving to match his deliberate casualness. "I thought you'd rather have roast beef or turkey sandwiches."

"Well, it's not what I'd rather have, but I'll settle for that," he sighed, pulling his pack forward and taking out the red checkered cloth she'd packed.

"If it has to be roast beef or turkey, which would you rather?" Laura asked.

"How about half of each?"

She nodded, understanding all too well that impulse to share.

As they ate, a mottled bird with a light head and a long beak tapped industriously on a nearby maple tree.

"I guess that's a woodpecker," Laura observed. "I wish I knew what kind."

"Actually, it's a yellow-bellied sapsucker."

Laura gave him a sideways glance. "You're making that up."

Brandon shook his head. "No. Scout's honor. A favorite, but slightly eccentric, uncle brought me a bird-identification book for my third birthday, and you know how kids are. I made my mother read it to me every night before I went to sleep. After a hundred or so repetitions, I had the damn thing memorized." He grinned. "If there were some cedar waxwings or red-breasted flycatchers around here, I'd point them out, too."

"Well, robins, blue jays and cardinals are about the

only birds I know. So I guess you can teach me a thing or two."

"Or two," he agreed.

"My favorite bedtime stories were Babar books," Laura mused, suddenly remembering her own childhood obsession.

"You mean that elephant who grew up to be king of the jungle?"

"Um-hum."

They spent the rest of the meal gleefully trading early memories. When they had finished their sandwiches, Brandon reached into his pack for a small white cardboard box.

"What's that?"

"The dessert I promised."

Opening the package, Laura discovered a wedge of cherry cheesecake and two plastic forks. Her eyes widened. He had remembered. "It's one of my favorites."

"I was hoping so." He cut off a piece and lifted it toward her lips. Laura accepted the offering, her eyes never leaving Brandon's face as she chewed appreciatively on the rich, creamy morsel topped by slightly tart cherry filling.

He broke off another piece with the same fork, brought it to his own lips and savored the combination of flavors just as she had. "You have very good taste," he complimented.

"Thank you."

Brandon continued to alternate bites between the two of them until the slice had disappeared.

"I guess we didn't need the extra fork after all," she murmured.

"No."

The intimacy of the shared dessert had made Laura aware of just how isolated they were down there. Not even noises from the distant highway reached them beside the rushing water of the stream. It was as though the rest of the world no longer existed, as though the two

of them and this protected valley were the only reality.
Laura couldn't help finding that thought a bit disconcert-
ing. She would be more comfortable, she realized, if she
shifted the focus of attention away from themselves.

"You should see this place later in the season," she
observed, casting a glance up and then down the stream.
"You won't believe how different it will look in a couple of
months. The ferns aren't even up yet—not to mention
the poison ivy," she added.

Brandon raised an eyebrow.

"Well, now you know the terrible secret," Laura
continued. "Poison ivy is a part of summer around here.
But if you wear heavy shoes and socks and stay out of
the worst patches, you'll be okay."

"I hope so." As he spoke, he stowed their trash in his
pack and refolded the tablecloth. Down on the broad
rock, the sun was pleasantly warm. In the trees, an
occasional bird burst into song. Brandon took off his
jacket and spread it behind Laura. "Time to relax before
we have to climb back out to civilization," he suggested.

"Is this a ploy so that you can have your wicked way
with me out here in the middle of nowhere?" she asked,
not quite able to keep her voice steady.

"Yes." As he spoke he pushed gently on her shoulder,
and with the other hand eased her down to a prone
position.

She looked up at him, half afraid and yet already
responding to the unmistakably possessive gesture with a
tingle of anticipation.

"But I promise not to be too wicked," he added, lying
down beside her and rolling over onto his stomach so
that his face hovered above hers, blocking out everything
except the blue canopy of the sky above him.

"Why?" she whispered.

"Because my strategy at this stage of the game is to
leave you wanting more."

"Is it a game, then?" she questioned, understanding
that it was her old familiar apprehension that kept the

conversation going, as though building a wall of meaningless syllables between them would somehow protect her.

"No, much more than a game," he amended, his own voice not quite steady now. Quickly he covered her lips with his own, so that her next words were lost in the mingling of their breath. Part of her craved the contact, even reveled in it, as his tongue teased the barrier of her teeth before boldly plunging beyond. And then his lips left hers to explore the line of her jaw, investigate the delicate curve of her ear, trail down the column of her throat. "Much better than even cherry cheesecake for dessert," he murmured, then raised his head to look down into her blue eyes.

That look melted her resistance and made her unconsciously curve her body into the warmth of his. She saw a fierce possessiveness in the depth of his ebony eyes, a possessiveness that would have frightened her except that it was tempered with an almost heartbreaking tenderness.

"Brandon." His name came as softly to her lips as a spring breeze caressing a bed of flowers. And then she was raising her hands to twine them around his neck and tangle them in the thick dark hair at the back of his head. The freedom to touch him like this was one of the pleasures she had come to crave over the past week.

He answered her gesture by clasping his own arms more tightly around her shoulders and finding her mouth with his again. This time, there was no way she could have held back her response. Her tongue mated with his, stroking and caressing. When at last he drew back slightly, they were both breathless. She could feel the pounding of her heart in her chest. Or was it his? They were pressed so tightly together that she didn't know where she ended and he began.

Brandon was all too aware of the flush that spread across her cheeks, the smoldering passion in her eyes. He wanted to lever himself on top of her, to sink into the softness of her welcoming body. And yet he knew from her initial hesitation that it was still much too soon for that.

The messages she was sending him were still mixed. Her body had made its decision. But her fear of intimacy was such an ingrained response that he knew one false move would send her scurrying back into the protective shell from which she had so recently emerged. Instead of following his desires, he rolled to his side, pulling her with him so that they lay barely touching at shoulder and hip. His hand played with a lock of her hair, glided across her cheek and moved farther down to stroke the ridge of her collarbone just visible at the open neck of her plaid shirt. And then he was unable to stop his hand from sliding lower to cup the warm swell of her breast.

He felt her quiver against him, heard her indrawn breath as he began to gently caress her. Neither of them spoke. But words would have been an intrusion now. He felt her breast swell and her nipple harden in response through the thin layers of fabric that separated his fingers from her body. He had half expected that she might draw away. Instead she closed her eyes and pressed her face against his chest.

He listened to the raggedness of her breathing, knowing that it was matched by his own. He knew that she wanted him. But it was even more important that she trust him.

Only by a supreme effort of will did he keep his fingers from undoing the buttons of her shirt. He ached to feel the warm skin of her breast against his hand, to discover the taste and texture of her aroused nipples with his mouth, to strip off both their shirts and pull her against his naked chest.

For a long heart-stopping moment, neither of them moved. And then he bent to kiss her cheek before sitting up.

"Well, so much for leaving *you* wanting more," he conceded. His throat was so constricted that he could barely get the words out.

They packed up their gear and left quickly after that. And they hardly spoke as they climbed up to the road or on the ride back to the house. Each was caught up in his own private thoughts.

"Listen," Brandon began as he pulled the Blazer up next to her car, "I've been neglecting my work for the past few days. But there's a report I have to get out before this weekend."

"You're right, I have been taking up a lot of your time," she shot back instantly. But before she could go on, he covered her hand with his own.

"Don't be so quick to jump to conclusions. I like having you take up my time. But even though I don't have to report to the office every day, I *am* supposed to be earning a living."

"You're right. I'm sorry," she murmured. All he had said was that he had to get some work done, and she had reacted like a hen with ruffled feathers. If she couldn't feel more secure than that, maybe she hadn't come as far as she thought.

"I have Sylvia to cover for me," she pointed out, as though thinking aloud. "But you're running things here all by yourself."

Brandon grinned. "I may not have a dragon working for me, but I'm not without resources. I do have a modem that connects my computer to the office in Chicago so I can use their research facilities. And my machine's got word-processing software." He stopped and thought for a moment. "I should be able to get that report out of the way in a couple of days of concentrated effort—so I can focus my attention on you again."

Laura leaned back against the seat and then watched curiously as he reached into the glove compartment and pulled out a folded section of the *Harperstown Gazette.*

"Change of subject," he announced as he handed the paper to Laura. Circled in red was a rectangular advertisement with tightly spaced copy.

"Sounds interesting, doesn't it?" he questioned. "Ever been to a country auction?"

"Are you kidding? My parents were auction freaks. They practically furnished their whole house with stuff they picked up that way. By the time I was seven, I was already bidding on books and toys."

"Well, I've never been, but I thought it would be a great way to pick up some 'furniture with character' for my empty house. Want to go with me Saturday evening? We could eat first and then go."

"Now I know you're really an auction tyro," Laura teased. "Part of the charm is the fried chicken and homemade pie. Besides, you want to get there early so you can have a look at the stuff for sale. There's no use bringing home a chest and then discovering that the drawer bottoms are ready to fall out."

Brandon raised an eyebrow. "If that's the case with most of the furniture, maybe I'd better try a more conventional route."

"It's not," Laura assured him. "But the operative rule is 'Buyer beware.'"

Now, after stepping out of the shower and drying herself off, Laura pulled a soft cranberry blouse and matching slacks out of her closet. Brandon was going to be surprised to see her wearing something besides work clothes, she thought as she laid the outfit on her quilt-covered bed and headed for the shower.

After toweling dry, she took more time than usual with her hair and makeup, applying soft pink blusher to her cheeks and light gray shadow to her eyelids. The first morning they'd met, Brandon had practically told her she looked like a kid. But that wasn't the effect she wanted to achieve tonight.

A knock at the front door interrupted her just as she

was giving her reflection a final inspection. After turning to check the fit of her slacks one last time, she hurried downstairs and threw open the door.

Brandon stood on the front porch. Like Laura, he had discarded his denims; he was clad in dark slacks, a tweed sports coat and a blue button-down shirt. For a moment she simply stood there looking at him, all at once overwhelmed by how much she had missed him during the past few days. She found herself drinking in every detail of his appearance—the way his thick hair curved over the tops of his ears, the strong line of his eyebrows, the very masculine shadow that he could never entirely erase from his cheeks no matter how recently he had shaved, the well-tailored fit of his jacket across his broad shoulders.

So absorbed was she that she didn't realize his eyes were devouring her just as hungrily. But when his dark gaze locked with her blue one, she felt a rush of feeling, as though she were flying a lighter-than-air craft suddenly caught in a warm, hidden updraft.

"Laura, I didn't know how much I'd miss you while I was working on that report." The roughened texture of his voice seemed to pull her forward as it always did. And before she knew it, she was enfolded in his arms, her body pressed tightly against the length of his. It was as though she were being cherished after a long separation. Yet the moment was over almost before it had begun.

Stepping back, he reached down and picked up a long white box that he'd set down on the porch before ringing the bell.

"For you," he said, holding it out.

"What's that?" Laura questioned.

"A present."

When she opened the box, she found a dozen exquisite blue and purple miniature irises. They looked so perfect that it took her a moment to realize they were made of silk.

"Oh, they're lovely," she breathed, touching one of

the soft blue petals. "But you didn't have to bring me anything."

"I very much wanted to bring you flowers this evening," he said. "But when I walked into the florist shop, I suddenly realized I'd never seen any cut ones in your office—or at your house, either—even though you own a garden center. So I got these instead."

She gazed up at him, touched by the gesture—and by his perception of her habits. How many men would have noticed that kind of detail? she wondered.

"You're right," she finally said. "I don't like to put real flowers in vases because once you've cut their stems, they start to die. But that won't happen with these beautiful things," she added.

"I should have known you'd have a reason like that."

"I know it's silly, really."

"No. Not silly at all."

Laura felt her cheeks redden slightly. She'd never told anyone about those particular feelings before. "Let me get something to put them in," she murmured, turning to the china closet in the corner. Bringing down a tall cut-glass pitcher, she carefully arranged the irises and placed the container in the middle of the sideboard. They looked handsome set off against the light blue of the wallpaper.

Turning back to Brandon, she smiled. "They're perfect for this room."

"I'm glad you think so." For a few seconds he stood very close to her. There was a warm intimacy to the moment, and she wondered fleetingly if he was going to take her in his arms again. But instead, he looked at his watch. "We're going to be late if we don't leave pretty soon," he advised.

"Yes."

"And if we don't leave right now, we may never get there at all."

Laura made no comment. Instead she collected her jacket and followed him out to the Blazer.

There were a million things they had to tell each other on the way to the auction—amusing or frustrating or simply interesting details of their daily lives that they had stored up.

Laura was still laughing over his account of how he'd fouled up his margins on the word processor and feared he was going to have to turn in his report as a two-inch-wide column running down five-hundred pages, when they pulled into the already crowded parking lot at the auction gallery.

"I see what you mean about getting here early," Brandon commented. "What did this place used to be, anyway?" he asked curiously as they entered the long room decked out with barn wood siding and massive rafters. All around the walls were framed pictures and mirrors, miscellaneous pieces of furniture and tables laden with glassware, silver and other knickknacks.

"It was built as a square-dance hall," Laura informed him. "But somehow the idea never caught on, so the gallery was able to pick up the place fairly reasonably. Let's get you a number first and then see what looks interesting," she added.

"A number?"

"Yes, they register all the buyers to make sure everybody pays up—and nobody goes home with the wrong box of antimacassars."

While Brandon stood in line, Laura put their coats on two seats near the middle of the room so they'd have a good view of both the auction block and the crowd.

After obtaining an index card with 117 written on the back in bold black numerals, Brandon rejoined Laura, who was already strolling among the crowd inspecting desks, chairs and washstands.

"That's a magnificent piece," he commented, pointing toward a large mahogany armoire with an inlaid front and high curved pediment.

"What do you think about using the middle section for a liquor cabinet and the drawers for linens?" he asked as he opened the cabinet and carefully inspected the doors and interior.

"Great idea."

Before settling down with fried chicken and cole slaw, they found several other items of interest, particularly an oval oak table and six chairs.

"Somebody's done a terrific job of refinishing this set," Laura informed him as she sat in one of the chairs. "And they're sturdy, too."

They ate their dinner during the early stages of the proceedings, accompanied by the rapid-fire spiel of the auctioneer, a man of hulking stature but great eloquence. He was unerringly able to point out the special virtue of each item brought to the front and held up for display by the gallery staff.

"I'm beginning to catch on to the buyer-beware part," Brandon whispered to Laura. "When that guy says a piece of china isn't signed but looks like Roseville or Haviland, he's doing it to create an impression."

Laura nodded. "But most people don't get carried away with the florid commentary. They understand the game—unless they get really excited about something they want," she amended as a woman in the next row waved her number card frantically to attract the auctioneer's attention.

Together they watched the impromptu drama and exchanged amused glances as the buyer was finally handed the antique shaving kit she had been vying for so furiously.

"You know," Brandon observed as the auctioneer accepted bids and counterbids on a set of iced-tea glasses, "some of these pieces look like they're going for practically nothing. And others get pushed way up beyond what I'd guess is their value—like that shaving kit."

"Um-hum. It all depends on who wants it—and for what. Take that pair, for example." As she spoke, Laura pointed out a gray-bearded man sitting next to a conservatively dressed woman on the other side of the room. "I've seen them before. They're both dealers. They've got a lot of money to spend, but they won't bid too high on any one item. That would wipe out their profit margin."

Brandon slid his arm around Laura. Even in this crowded room filled with tobacco smoke and the din of the audience above the auctioneer's singsong, they were somehow a little island unto themselves. As the action swirled around them, they exchanged comments and laughing observations.

It wasn't until the end of the evening that Brandon entered the fray. On the block was a small oak washstand that he had admired earlier. But when the bidding went to ninety dollars he put his numbered card back in his breast pocket.

Turning to Laura, he shook his head. "I guess I lost my nerve. But it seemed too much to pay for a piece like that."

"It has nothing to do with nerve. You're right about the price. Save your money for something you really want."

When two husky attendants pulled the armoire away from the wall, Laura saw Brandon's eyes light up. This time, the bidding quickly went to $450—with only one dealer and Brandon still in the running.

"Shall I drop out?" he whispered when the auctioneer asked for $475.

"No!" Unable to contain her own excitement, Laura snatched the number card from her companion's hand and waved it at the auctioneer when he glanced in their direction once again.

"I have four seventy-five," he acknowledged, looking pointedly across at their rival.

Laura held her breath as the man hesitated for a moment and then gave a small shake of the head.

"Four seventy-five going once, going twice, going three times," he intoned, "Sold to number one seventeen."

Laura looked at the card in her hand. "Oh. I'm sorry. If you didn't want to pay that much . . ."

"I like your style," Brandon assured her. "And I think the armoire's worth the money."

When the table and chairs came up, Laura contained her own excitement and allowed Brandon to do the honors. This time there was no thought of dropping out. And at the end of the bidding he found he had made another major purchase.

"Want to leave before I bankrupt myself?" he asked Laura.

"Maybe we'd better."

After he had paid by check and arranged for delivery, they returned to the Blazer.

"I think I've caught auction fever," Brandon commented as he started the engine.

"Well, it's easy to treat that malady. We just have to go again."

"You've got a deal."

5

On the way home, they continued their animated discussion of the evening.

"That was really quite a show," Brandon commented as they pulled into her long, rutted driveway. "Better than television, anyway."

"And more fun than a regular furniture store," Laura added.

She looked up fondly into Brandon's dark eyes. "You know, I haven't had so much fun in a long time."

"Me neither," he agreed, giving her shoulder a quick squeeze.

"And part of it was seeing the whole thing from your point of view," Laura added. "I've been going to auctions for so many years that I take them for granted, but tonight you gave me a new perspective."

For a moment she hesitated with her fingers on the door handle. "Want to come in for a cup of coffee?" she asked, suddenly reluctant to end the evening.

"I was hoping you'd ask."

As they stepped into the living room, Brandon looked around with new interest. "You know, I'll bet I can pick out which of your furnishings are auction purchases," he observed. "What about that gateleg end table?"

"Right."

"And that brass floor lamp?"

Laura grinned. "Nope. Mom had banished that to the attic. I just brought it down and polished it up."

As he continued to look around, she hung up their coats on the hall rack and then headed for the kitchen to start the coffee. Suddenly she was feeling a bit nervous.

For the past few hours they had been essentially isolated from the rest of the people in the crowded auction gallery, as though the two of them were sharing a private, intimate world. But now that they were really alone so late in the evening, it took an effort to keep her hand from trembling slightly as she got down the canister of dark, aromatic beans.

Before she could fill the percolator with water, Brandon had come into the kitchen. For a moment he stood looking at her, his eyes intense. Then he crossed to the sink and turned off the water.

"Don't waste good coffee," he advised huskily. "That's not really what I want tonight."

"It isn't?" she found herself asking. It was a stupid question, for on one level, she had really known that all along.

"No."

It took only a moment for him to close the distance between them and pull her into his arms. And then his lips were seeking hers in a kiss that spoke more eloquently than any words.

"Laura, I've been thinking about holding you like this for days," he groaned, his arms tightening around her shoulders and his lips leaving hers to trace a random path across her eyebrows, her cheek, the bridge of her nose.

She had been thinking about it too, secretly longing for it, if the truth be known. She molded her hands to the back of his head and brought his lips back to the eager warmth of hers. The taste of him was intoxicating. She felt as if a warm, smoky mist enveloped her very being, clouding her mind and robbing it of conscious thought.

For a few moments, Brandon seemed lost in the delights of the kiss as well. He was hungry for every nuance. And as his tongue explored the texture of her lips and the warm, velvet cavity beyond, she heard his sigh of satisfaction.

But there was more he wanted, much more. She felt him shift her body so that his hand could find her breasts. And this time her response left no doubt that she wanted that contact, too. The soft mounds strained forward at his touch. And as their sensitive peaks hardened in answer to his loving attentions, she was unable to hold back a wordless, inarticulate little cry of pleasure.

Brandon's own response was instantaneous. His fingers found the buttons of her blouse, and as he slid each one open, his lips followed their path. Tenderly he kissed the newly discovered territory.

After a long, heart-stopping moment, he raised his head to look into her eyes, his burning gaze seeking and finding an answering fire there.

Her breath caught in her throat as his index finger dipped inside the lacy cup of her bra, gliding across her quivering flesh with a maddeningly erotic stroke that seemed to turn her bones to liquid. All at once she found that she was forced to cling to him in order to keep her footing. No one had made her feel this way before, and it was hard to cope with the sensation.

With one hand, Brandon freed her shirt from the waistband of her slacks. Reaching behind her, he stroked his fingers across the silky skin of her back and then reached to unhook the clasp of her bra. At the same time, his other hand slid down to the lower part of her body, pulling her more firmly against the evidence of his own swelling desire. He had warned himself to go slowly with Laura. But that had just become impossible. He had been reining in his own needs and desires for much too long. And now, all at once he wanted her with a fierce desperation that could no longer be denied. It was impossible for him not to move his hips against hers, silently urging her complete response.

Until that moment, Laura had been craving his closeness and at the same time reacting almost instinctively to the desires and sensations he was weaving around and through her—without considering where they would ultimately lead. But now reality intruded. Her half-closed eyes snapped open. Suddenly she was all too aware of her unencumbered breasts and the disturbingly provocative movement of Brandon's lower body against hers. Everything was happening so fast. And all at once she realized she wasn't yet prepared for what was inevitably going to happen next.

"Brandon, please," she protested. But he mistook the intent of her words and only pulled her closer, his hand pushing her bra aside so that he could cup her breast once more.

"Please . . . don't," she tried again, this time pushing desperately against his shoulder. But she might as well have been pushing against a full-grown oak tree for all the good it did. Frantic now, she thumped the heel of her hand against his chest.

His passion-clouded eyes finally focused on her face. "What do you mean, 'don't'?"

She shook her head miserably. "Please, I can't. Not yet. I just can't."

His gaze never leaving her face, he took a step backwards. "A moment ago I thought you were leading me to believe you could," he said thickly, his eyes still dark with unfulfilled passion.

Laura bit her lip and pulled the gaping front of her shirt closed over her unhooked bra. How could she explain the trapped feeling, the fear, the certain knowledge of what it would mean if she surrendered this last part of herself and then lost him?

"Remember," she began in a small voice, "you said you wouldn't push me, that you'd give me time."

He seemed to consider her words carefully. "I thought I had. But if you're not ready *now*, maybe you never will be."

She looked away, desperately fighting back tears that blurred her vision. He was right, of course. All through the evening there had been a warm thread of desire pulling them closer together. And just now she had given him every reason to believe that she wanted him. And she did. That was precisely what made things so difficult. She wanted to explain, wanted to tell him how much it had cost her to come this far, how precious the time they had spent together was to her. How hard it had been to fight the fear that it would all come to an end. But the words stuck in her throat.

"Well?" The syllable was a sardonic challenge, a harsh reproach.

She knew now that it would be impossible to speak. If she tried, she would break down in front of him. And the proud, lonely part of her that had been immured for so long must avoid that at all costs.

"Well?" he repeated.

But she only kept her face averted, fighting to hold on to the last tattered shreds of her control.

"All right, Laura," he rasped, "I guess there isn't anything more to say, is there?"

Turning on his heel, he left the kitchen. A moment later she heard the front door slam shut.

The sound seemed to reverberate through the house, but it was soon replaced by her own weeping.

The leaden sky matched Laura's mood as she looked out her office window one afternoon a week later. Brandon hadn't called since he'd turned so abruptly and left her standing in the kitchen the night of the auction. But then, she hadn't expected him to. She might as well get used to the idea that their personal relationship was over.

She hadn't been able to make herself pick up the phone and call him. That would have been too much like begging. And Laura Carson didn't beg. But she had taken advantage of the one avenue of communication that was still open. Earlier in the week she had sent her crew out to start excavating for the stairway and lay footings for the deck. But Brandon, who had been so anxious to finally get the work started, hadn't made any comment to her about it—or anything else.

For the past week, she had essentially been filling up her time with paper work and jobs her clerks could just as easily have handled. It had been impossible for her to do anything more creative. Every sketch she made ended up in the trash basket beside her desk. Every artistic thought was stillborn.

Sylvia had noticed her bleak mood and loss of appetite at once. But Laura had turned away the woman's first anxious questions with a tone of voice that had made it clear she didn't want to talk about her personal life.

Come on, she urged herself. You pulled yourself together once. You can do it again. You didn't even let the man drag you to bed before he discarded you this time.

The thought made her cover her eyes with her hands. She hadn't thought about *that* in a long time—about the few frantic trysts she and Arthur had "enjoyed" during their brief engagement. Or at least, she reminded herself bitterly, he had said he'd enjoyed them. For her there had simply been the desire to please, nothing more. The actual experience had left her cold.

Was that why she had been so afraid to let down the final barriers with Brandon? she asked herself now. Was it her fear that his lovemaking would leave her cold again, providing one more stinging proof of her inadequacy as a woman?

No, she hadn't really believed that would be true this

time. Even though she'd thought herself in love with Arthur, she'd never responded to his self-centered lovemaking as she had to Brandon.

Instead, she had felt her response to Brandon growing and building like the pressure of raging water behind a weakened dam. She had been afraid of what would happen when that metaphorical dam burst and all her naked emotions came pouring forth.

Laura's thoughts were interrupted by a knock at the door.

"Come in," she called, looking up to see Tim Warfield standing in the doorway. An electrical contractor, he was one of the leaders of the Harperstown Business Association. About ten years older than Laura, he'd been the one to get her involved in several civic committees. There was a time a few years ago when she'd had the feeling that Tim wanted to make their relationship more personal. But she'd had no real problem resisting his blond good looks, and he'd eventually married someone else. Their friendship had stayed intact, however, and their respect for each other had remained high.

The last time they'd worked together, it had been to come up with a summer youth employment plan. Laura had been a key member of the planning group. Tim had done the legwork, canvassing the business community for funds to get the program going.

"Hi, Tim. What brings you here?" Laura asked, assuming that he had some new pet project he wanted to interest her in.

"I wanted to find out what you know about General Development Corporation—and Brandon McGuire."

Laura couldn't help being startled by the completely unexpected question. She had just been thinking about Brandon rather intimately, after all. But she certainly didn't want to talk about the man. "I don't know much about the company," she hedged, knowing that Tim had probably come for information because he'd heard about her association with Brandon. That was almost inevitable in a city as small as Harperstown.

Tim confirmed her supposition. "Several people told me you might be a good source of information about McGuire."

Laura shrugged with deliberate casualness. "I met him when he came in for a landscape consultation—and we talked a little bit about the conference center he was planning downtown. But I probably don't know more than you do," she claimed, hoping that Tim would take the hint and leave.

He only nodded, and sat down in the chair opposite Laura's desk, as though waiting for her to continue. When she didn't, he cleared his throat. "You know, a lot of people are concerned about that project."

"Don't you think the downtown area needs revitalization?" Laura questioned, pushing her chair away from the desk and leaning back slightly.

"Yes, but there are questions about whether General Development is the right group to do it. In the first place, they're outsiders, and they don't really have a stake in the community."

Laura had suspected that this kind of opposition to Brandon's project would surface, but not from someone as progressive as Tim. "So who raised the issue?" she asked.

He looked slightly embarrassed. "Actually, Hal Kramer."

Laura rolled her eyes. A picture of the man in question, with his moon face, thin wisps of brown hair combed across a shiny bald pate, and perpetually rumpled suit, leaped into her mind. Hal Kramer seemed so fundamentally unimposing. Yet he was a key force in the old guard Harperstown Business Association. His views rarely coincided with hers and Tim's. In fact, they'd had to overcome Kramer's opposition to the youth employment program—and a number of other projects they both considered worthwhile. "Don't tell me you and Kramer are in agreement about something?" she asked.

Tim leaned forward earnestly. "This time I think he's got a point," he said. "Why don't you have a look at this?" he added, handing Laura a sheaf of typed pages enclosed in a blue binder.

"What is it?" she asked, opening the cover. And then her eyes widened. At the top of the first page were the words "General Development Preliminary Harperstown Report, Official and Confidential."

"Where did you get this?" she inquired.

Tim seemed a bit disconcerted by the question. "Hal got a copy—I'm not sure where. But that's, uh, not really important. You can read the whole thing later. But you might want to look at the first two pages now. They're the executive summary."

Laura ran her eyes down the closely spaced paragraphs. The beginning of the report was a catalog of the pitfalls General Development was likely to encounter in setting up the conference center Brandon had described. It pointed out the traffic and parking problems the complex might generate, the inadequacy of the local sewage treatment plant to handle the additional load, and the number of established businessmen who would be displaced by the facility. The last paragraph assessed the number of historic townhouses that might have to be razed. It was far larger than Brandon had indicated.

"Are you sure this is accurate and that it really comes from General Development?" she asked, her brow wrinkling. This was certainly not the view Brandon had given her of the project. If Hal Kramer had come to her with the information, Laura might have been able to convince herself that he'd made it up himself. But she knew Tim well enough to be sure that he'd never stoop to such tactics.

"I had it verified. It's from their own planning division, all right," Tim assured her. "Hal is hoping you'll be able to come to a meeting we're having in the next week or so to prepare for the zoning hearing," he added.

"I—I'll have to think about it," Laura murmured. She was having trouble assimilating what she'd just read.

They talked for a few more minutes, but Laura was barely able to concentrate on the conversation.

Mercifully, Tim finally stood up. "Well, I'd better get going. Give me a call when you have a chance to read the whole thing."

When Tim had left, Laura looked over the report, going beyond the summary at the beginning to the more detailed pages beyond. As she read, the pain she had been feeling all week began to find a focus.

Since Brandon's abrupt departure after the auction, she had been hoping that he would call to repair the breach in their relationship. But he hadn't. And while she had allowed herself to feel hurt over his apparent rejection, she had been repressing her anger at the way he'd treated her.

Now she couldn't keep that anger from washing over her. Brandon had pushed her into a personal relationship against her strong and persistent objections. On very short acquaintance, he had gone to great lengths to get her to open up with him. And then he had simply walked out of her life like some anthropologist who was through with his research study.

But, of course, she couldn't throw any of that in his face. She was too proud for such self-revelations. And deep down, she knew she didn't want to give him the chance to hurt her again.

However, this damning report was an entirely different matter. It said nothing about Brandon McGuire as a person—or her relationship with him. It simply raised serious doubts about his business ethics. And that gave her a completely different reason to be resentful of him. He hadn't just hoodwinked her on a personal level, he had lied to her about his plans in Harperstown. And the evidence was here in black and white—with his company's name blazoned across the top of the first page.

Laura glanced out the window. The sun was low in the sky and it was already close to quitting time. She pushed back her chair, picked up her pocketbook and went to ask Sylvia to take charge of closing up for the day. Now that she had a legitimate excuse to let Mr. Brandon McGuire know what she thought of him, she was going to take it.

Twenty minutes later, wearing her righteous indignation like a heavy cloak, she climbed out of her car and marched toward the front of his house.

"Laura!" he exclaimed as he threw open the double doors.

He'd been angry and hurt Friday night, and he'd wanted her to know it before he'd stamped out of her kitchen. On the way home, he'd decided he couldn't open himself up for that kind of dismissal again. But it had taken only a few days of being without Laura to realize he was only kidding himself. He had to try again. The trouble was, after the way he'd left, he hadn't been sure how to approach her. And yet here she was now, standing on his doorstep. It was certainly more than he had dared to hope for—and more than he deserved.

His first impulse was to pull her thankfully into his arms, until he caught the expression on her face. She hadn't come to make peace between them, as he had dared to let himself hope. She was angry.

For a moment, Laura stood looking at him. She had almost forgotten how strongly she responded to him on a physical level. And now her breath caught in her throat as her eyes swept over his lean, well-muscled frame and chiseled features. He was dressed as usual in jeans and a button-down shirt. What was she doing here, really? she wondered. She had to force herself to hold on to her anger.

"Laura," he repeated, "what's the matter?"

"As if you don't know," she snorted. As she spoke, she waved the feasibility report in his face.

"What's that?" he asked, taking the papers from her hand. Then he stepped backwards so that she could enter the foyer. "Maybe you'd better come in so we can talk," he added.

She followed him down the hall to the living room, noting absently that the auction furniture had been delivered—along with a square modern couch covered in a burgundy velvet, and an oriental rug.

"Why don't you sit down?" Brandon offered, taking his own advice. But Laura chose to stand, glaring down at him. Shrugging, he turned over the stack of papers and scanned the introductory paragraphs while Laura paced back and forth in front of the windows.

Finally he looked up, puzzled. "This is the preliminary report General Development did on the conference center site," he confirmed. "But it's confidential information. How did you get hold of it?"

"That's really not important," Laura shot back. "The important thing is that it paints quite a different picture of your plans from the one you gave me."

"Of course," Brandon agreed evenly. "That's why it's a *preliminary* report."

"Is it really?" Laura challenged sarcastically. "Then what about the traffic problems? What about the parking? The sewage? What about those historic townhouses you assured me you were going to incorporate into your complex?"

Brandon shook his head. He was still trying to deal with Laura on a rational level. "That report represents our very earliest thinking about the Harperstown project. It went into every pitfall we could conceive of—in great detail. Naturally, we had to spell out all the potential problems before we could come up with solutions. It was quite a job. But we've been able to deal with every one of those factors in a positive way."

Laura simply stared down at him with narrowed eyes.

"If I had the final report explaining how we solved the problems," Brandon continued, "I'd show it to you. But it's in Chicago being reviewed by company management right now. However, you're welcome to see my draft if you like."

"Of course you don't have the final report," she shot back. "How convenient for you. And what about that offer you made me about designing your damn courtyard? Was that some sort of bribe?"

"Laura, what's the matter with you?" He had never seen Laura Carson like this, and he was having trouble coming to grips with the woman who stood glaring down at him. "You can't seriously believe I'd lie to you, can you?" he asked, getting to his feet and coming toward her. But when she took a step backwards, he halted too.

"It wouldn't be the first time." She hadn't intended to say anything like that. The accusation had simply slipped out.

Brandon's features darkened. So far he had been able to remain relatively calm. But she had just pushed him too far. "And just what is that supposed to mean?" he demanded, spacing the words evenly as though he were trying to reason with an angry child instead of a mature woman.

"If you don't already know, I don't think my telling you would do any good." She hurled the words at him like a javelin. Was she really saying these things? one small corner of her mind wondered. She didn't recognize herself in the woman shouting accusations at Brandon like a wronged heroine in a soap opera. And yet it was as though all the years of repression, of smothered feelings, were finally finding their outlet in this one violent outburst.

There was no way Brandon could really grasp what was happening, either. "Laura, what in the hell's going on here?" he began, his features a mixture of perplexity and anger.

But she was so wound up now that she simply couldn't stop. Hands on her hips, she glared at him. "You think you can come in here and sweep the people of Harperstown off their feet—just the way you swept me off my feet," she shouted. "And then what? Are you going to try to screw them just the way you tried to screw me?"

The words were followed by complete silence. It took a moment for her to realize what she'd said. And with the realization, she felt a dark flush spread across her cheeks. Suddenly she could hardly breathe. All she knew was that she had to get out of there before she made an even bigger fool of herself. She turned on her heel and fled back down the hall and out the front door.

She was just pulling open the door to her car when he caught up with her.

"Laura, I can't let you leave like this." As he spoke, he grabbed her by the shoulder.

"Take your hand off me."

"No."

With all the strength at her command, she smacked him across the face.

For a moment she stood there staring at him, watching the marks of her fingers darken on his cheek. But before she could turn away, he had picked her up and started back to the house.

Briefly, she feared retaliation. But his reaction was not what she had expected. "For God's sake, I'm not going to let you go like this," he repeated. She was too caught up in her own swirling emotions to understand the note of panic in his voice—or to take in the look of sheer desperation on his face.

In fact, for Laura, there was no control, no real conscious thought left. The only thing she knew was that she had to get away from this scene she had created. There was no way she was going to quietly let him carry her back inside. Operating on some basic level of self-preservation, Laura began to kick and struggle. But Brandon wasn't going to give in either. And though her strength came from a kind of mindless frenzy, he was by far the more powerful of the two. Doggedly but gently, he subdued her flailing arms and legs at considerable cost to his own person. He carried her back inside the house, slamming the door shut with his foot.

He marched into the living room and sat down heavily on the couch, still holding his struggling burden.

"All right," he rasped, holding her tightly against his chest. "Fight me if it will make you feel better."

Laura's reaction was a muffled sob. Part of her had already given up the physical contest. But she couldn't admit it yet. And so she kept struggling, pitting her strength against Brandon's until she finally fell forward in exhaustion against his chest.

Hot tears stung her eyes. She struggled to hold them in check and lost.

"It's all right," he soothed again, cradling her shoulders and smoothing her hair. "Go ahead and cry."

But the fury and frustration that had raged inside her had already spent itself in angry combat. There were not many tears.

Sensing that she had quieted, Brandon shifted her weight so that his eyes could meet hers. It wasn't a contact that Laura welcomed.

"I haven't lied to you about the conference center. We *have* come up with solutions to those problems," he said. "But we both know that all this isn't really about my company's plans in Harperstown," he added gently. "It's about us. I've hurt you. And, although I know it doesn't seem that way to you, that was the last thing I wanted to do."

She forced herself not to turn away. He was right. But the hurt was still there. "Why should I believe you?" she whispered.

She saw deep pain cloud his features, saw him hesitate and take a steadying breath as though fighting to get control of his own emotions. "Because you're the only woman I've cared about since my wife died, Laura," he said very quietly.

The statement was delivered in a flat and emotionless tone, as though he were talking about someone else. But she understood why. Wasn't she the master at deadening anguish with mental anesthetic?

He spoke of caring, and yet she felt his words as one might feel a knife wound, like a hot pain slicing through her chest. She knew that it was his hurt she was taking into herself. For a timeless moment, neither one of them spoke.

"How long?" she finally managed.

"Almost two years," he said in the same flat voice. "At the beginning, I wanted to smash things." For the first time since they had started this discussion, his voice took on some of its usual color. "But that didn't last very long. Most of that time, I think I was trying to work myself to death."

She nodded. She could understand that, too.

"I guess this Harperstown project was what started to bring me out of it. I thought I'd never really care about anything again. But it was exciting. A new concept. A new beginning. I got interested in it—really interested."

As he spoke, he lifted her gently from his lap and got up. She watched as he crossed to the window and stood looking out over the valley. "That's why my boss sent me here to handle everything right from the beginning," he went on. "Henry never said so, but he knew how much this project meant to me."

For seemingly endless moments, Laura watched the tense set of his shoulders and neck. Now she longed to get up and go to him, to throw her arms around him and take away his pain. But if he had wanted that, she reasoned, he wouldn't have put the distance of the room between them.

"I suppose I'd better tell you the rest of it," he finally said, his back still to her, his voice thick and gravelly. She saw him raise a hand and press his fingers against his temple as he spoke.

"You don't—" she tried to interrupt, but he cut her off.

"Yes I do," he said fiercely, his voice so thick with emotion now that his words slurred together. "I should have trusted you enough to tell you a long time ago."

He paused for a moment and then forced himself to continue. "Janie and I had been married four years and we'd just had our first child—a boy, Jason. She was depressed after the baby. Couldn't seem to snap out of it. She wasn't taking care of the house. She wasn't taking care of the baby. She wasn't taking care of me. Most days, she wasn't even bothering to get dressed in the morning."

She wanted to stop him, because somehow she thought she knew what was coming. But he pressed on relentlessly.

"Finally one evening after the housekeeper had gone home, I got angry about it. We had a fight. She accused me of not loving her anymore, of not understanding. She took Jason and left in the car to go to her mother's. But they never got there. She was speeding and hit a bridge abutment. So you see, in a way, it was my fault."

"Brandon, no," Laura choked out. She had to go to him now. She was across the room, folding her arms around him, before she even knew she had gotten off the sofa. "You weren't driving that car. How can you hold yourself responsible?"

"But I let her go. I practically sent her away. That's why I couldn't let you leave a little while ago when you were so angry." All at once she understood the note of panic she had heard in his voice and the desperation she had seen in his face.

"Brandon, it wasn't your fault," she repeated, looking up and catching the glint of tears in his eyes. Now she knew why he had been standing with his back to her.

She heard him sigh. "You're right. Intellectually, I've come to understand that. But it doesn't make it any easier."

There was nothing she could do but pull him tightly against her body, trying with her closeness to comfort him. He had told her that afternoon in her office that he'd been hurt in the past. Now she finally understood what had happened to him. And she realized, too, that it was her own emotional outburst that had wrung the telling of it from him in such a painful way.

For a moment his arms hung limply at his sides, but then slowly they came up to clasp her shoulders. Some of the tension went out of her, and she rested her head against his chest, listening to the rapid but steady beat of his heart.

"How do you feel?" she finally asked, knowing that the emotional strain of the past half hour might well be having some physical effect on him.

He gave a hollow laugh. "Actually, I've got one hell of a headache. So much for male invincibility."

Laura had been feeling helpless. Suddenly there was something she could do for Brandon. "Let me get you some aspirin," she offered.

"Really, you don't have to," he began. But she could tell that the denial was only halfhearted. The scene had drained his emotional resources.

She found aspirin in her purse and brought it to him with a glass of water. He was sitting on the sofa now, his fingers against his brow again.

After he had swallowed the tablets, Laura drew the drapes, darkening the room. "Why don't you put your feet up for a little while," she suggested.

This time, he took the advice without objecting. Laura sat down beside him, massaging his temples with her fingertips. After a few moments, she felt his body relax and his breathing become more regular.

"That feels good," he said.

"I'm glad."

She continued to soothe him with her fingers and with softly murmured words.

He seemed on the verge of drifting off to sleep when his eyes opened again. "Will you be here when I get up?" he asked simply.

"Yes."

6

Laura sat down on the rug beside the couch, her face only inches from Brandon's. The impulse to reach out and stroke his eyebrow or the curve of his lips was almost overwhelming. But she was afraid to wake him now. For long, quiet moments she sat there, looking at him in the semidarkness, fascinated by the oval shadows of his lashes against his cheek and the way his lips were parted slightly.

But the emotional turmoil of the past few hours had been draining for her as well as for him. By slow degrees, her eyelids grew heavy. And without realizing what was happening, she put her head down on the cushion beside him and drifted off into a light sleep.

She didn't know how much time had passed, but she knew what woke her. It was the touch of Brandon's finger as it lightly traced the outline of her lips, just as she had wanted to touch him. Her eyes fluttered open to find him lying on his side facing her, his gaze warm upon her sleep-softened features.

"Laura?"

In answer, she reached out slender arms in a gesture as old as time and pulled him close, letting her body tell him what words were inadequate to express.

His own arms tightened around her shoulders. And then he shifted so that he could pull her up beside him on the couch. For several moments, he simply held her as though he were afraid she might vanish. But she remained solid and warm and pliant in his arms, her body quickening to his embrace. His fingers stroked her cheek, and then moved down to the base of her throat, finding the pulse that had begun to beat rapidly and insistently.

She knew he felt the telltale pounding, but he had sensed her arousal before and been disappointed in her withdrawal. She wanted no misunderstandings now.

"Brandon, make love to me," she whispered.

Drawing back slightly, he searched her face, his dark gaze capturing her blue one. "Are you sure?"

"Yes."

"Laura!"

For a moment ripe with anticipation, she felt his warm breath upon her lips. And then his mouth, firm and sweet, covered hers. The kiss began as tenderly as spring, and Laura opened to it like a flower unfurling bright petals to the sun. In one blazing instant, all the pain and fear she had felt that day, had felt for eons, was swept away like an ice jam in an April thaw. This man had trusted her enough to share the most painful episode in his life. How could she not return that trust now?

He sensed the naked emotion behind her response, and his mouth seemed to meld and fuse with hers, turning gentle spring to the sultry heat of summer. His tongue plunged into the warm, mysterious cavern beyond her teeth, then drew back to repeat the calculated assault with another deep, thrusting stroke, and another.

A week ago, the potency of that kiss would have frightened Laura. Now she welcomed and surrendered to it gladly.

And then, suddenly, it was she who became the aggressor. Her tongue darted forward to tease the corners of his lips. His groan of pleasure made her grow even bolder. Before she could give herself time to reconsider, she was exploring the serrated line of his teeth and the warm, velvety interior of his mouth. The taste and textures of him were intoxicating. When she finally drew back, she was breathless, and so was he.

She saw the passion in his dark eyes as his gaze caressed her face. And all at once she wanted him to know exactly what he meant to her and how much she trusted him now.

"Don't you think this would be a good time to move to your bedroom?" she asked, her eyes never leaving his.

He nodded. But he still hesitated.

"Brandon, this time I really am sure," she whispered.

He kissed her again. And then, hand in hand, they started down the darkened hall.

She caught only a quick impression of the sparsely furnished room. But her eyes noted the wide bed that commanded one wall. The blinds were open and moonlight bathed the room in a soft, magical radiance. Even nature, it seemed, was conspiring to make this first time of theirs together special.

They stood facing each other in the pale light for a moment before his hands reached for her again.

"No, let me," she whispered. Taking a step backwards, she loosened the bottom of her shirt from the waistband of her jeans and began to slide open the buttons, her eyes locked with Brandon's once more. When the shirt hung loose, she pulled her arms out of the sleeves and dropped the garment onto the floor. She stood before him, her breasts confined only by the all-but-transparent fabric of her lace-edged bra.

Brandon didn't say a word, but she heard his indrawn breath and saw the heat smoldering in his eyes as her hands reached behind her to the bra's clasp. Quickly, before she could lose her nerve, she unhooked the wispy garment and sent it to join the shirt.

Brandon's hot gaze was like a physical caress against her skin. In response, she felt her breasts swell and her nipples pout toward him. "I knew you'd be beautiful like this," he whispered hoarsely. It took a supreme effort of will to keep his hands clenched at his sides. But he could see by the determined look in her eyes that she wasn't finished.

Her breasts swayed tantalizingly as she moved to his side and reached for the front of his shirt. As she had done with her own, she slowly slid the buttons open one by one, then tugged the fabric from the waistband of his pants.

Almost timidly now, her hand reached to smooth back the fabric, caressing the springy mat of dark hair on his chest as she did so.

That was too much for Brandon. In one swift motion, he pulled her against him and stepped backwards toward the bed, tumbling the two of them over so that at last they lay prone, her body firmly on top of his.

He grinned at her look of surprise. And then his arms wrapped themselves even more tightly around her, pressing her breasts against his chest as his hands caressed the silky skin of her back.

"Laura, Laura, you feel so good," he groaned, the sandpaper in his voice sending a shiver down her spine. "You don't know how I've dreamed of holding you like this."

She pressed her face into his hard shoulder, acutely aware of the prickles of sensation created by his chest hair against her breasts. But she was even more burningly aware of the hard evidence of his desire where her hips were cradled against his.

She felt his hands chart a trail down her naked back to the still-clothed swell of her rounded bottom so that he could press her more firmly against himself. And this time there was no thought of denying the answering response of her own feminine arousal. With a little sob, she wrapped her arms around his neck and sought his lips with her own again.

As the long, drugging kiss ended, she felt him roll her over so that their positions were reversed. When he drew away from her, she whimpered in protest. But it was only so that he could unfasten her jeans. Raising her hips, she helped him remove the unwanted garment, along with her lacy panties. And then he was quickly stripping off the rest of his own clothing. When he pulled her back into his arms, there was nothing between their bodies but the hot, electric tension of their desire.

She imagined herself ready for his ultimate embrace, but he had only begun to show her what sensual pleasure meant. With slow, ardent attentions, he set about to rouse her until her need matched his. His lips sought her breasts, sucking and teasing the nipples until her whole body quivered with fiery longing. His hands made a slow, exploring journey from her shoulder to her hips and then caressed their way across her thighs to the warm, waiting core of her femininity.

She felt herself turn liquid as he stroked and caressed her.

"Brandon, please," she begged, arching desperately against him. She had sensed instinctively that she would come alive at his touch. But she had never imagined it could be like *this*.

"Please," she repeated.

His eyes were dark, glowing coals as he covered her body with his own, parting her legs with one of his. His lips found hers, and at the same time, in one fluid movement, he entered her.

Her tiny gasp was almost lost against his lips. But he heard.

"Did I hurt you?" he asked urgently.

"No," she lied. It had been such a long time, that it was almost as though she had never done this before.

But Brandon sensed her uncertainty. He paused for a

moment, giving her time to adjust to the feel of him inside her. Then, cautiously, he thrust forward to deepen the embrace.

"Oh, Laura, this feels so damn good," he sighed.

"Yes," she answered timidly. She hadn't expected conversation now, and yet with Brandon, it seemed right.

For several heartbeats he looked down at her warmly. And then he began to slowly rock his hips.

"Laura, move with me," he urged after a moment. And she found that she could. Her body followed the rhythm he set as naturally as thunder follows lightning. But there were no words to describe the tight knot of intensity that built as her body rocked with him. It was as though she were spiraling upward in an ever-tightening coil of pleasure.

She didn't hear the soft moans of ecstasy that escaped her lips as she approached the summit of her upward climb, didn't know that her fingernails dug into his shoulders or that her face was a study in rapture.

She only knew that when the blazing climax came, she called his name, and that a moment later she heard him answer her with the same desperate joy.

For an endless moment they simply clung together. And then Brandon stirred and kissed her cheek.

"That was incredible, in case you didn't know," he murmured, rolling to his side and pulling her with him so that he could nestle her body against his.

"It was for me," she whispered shyly. She wanted to tell him that she had never imagined it could be so wonderful, but she couldn't quite find the words. Instead she gave him a fiercely tender kiss.

His hand reached up to stroke her hair and cradle her head against his chest. She snuggled more closely against him, seeking his warmth. Now that their passion was spent, she was suddenly aware that the room was chilly.

Brandon felt it too. "I hate to move," he groaned, "but that's the only way to get under the covers." Swinging his feet over the side of the bed, he stood and, unconcerned about his nakedness, began to pull back the blanket and sheet. Laura gazed up at him from under her lashes, still shy but nevertheless anxious to take in this view of his unclothed body. The mat of crisp chest hair, which had brushed her skin as he embraced her, caught her attention first and drew her gaze down to his tapered waist and beyond. Hastily she raised her eyes, trying to take in the total picture.

He was trim and firm and flat of belly, she noted, without an ounce of extra flesh, and the muscles of his upper arms seemed to ripple as he turned the covers down. Pausing for a moment, he grinned. And Laura could tell that he had caught her watching him. But instead of teasing her about it, he simply held the covers so that she could slip under. Then he climbed back in beside her.

"That's much better," he growled, settling her in his arms again and curving his body protectively around hers once more.

"What time is it, do you suppose?" she asked, fishing for something to say in this totally unfamiliar situation.

"Much too late for you to go home." As he spoke, he pulled her back firmly against his chest and hugged her close. She felt his lips brush her hair before moving on to the side of her neck and the delicate curl of her ear. "Besides, I've found I like waking up next to you. And so I intend to keep you captive here, at least till morning."

Laura reveled in the warmth of his embrace. For her it was an incredible experience to be this close to another human being, and she wanted to savor it. She felt safe and cherished in Brandon's arms. Part of her wanted this night to go on forever, although she knew that was an impossible wish.

For a long time, he simply held her in the moonlight, his hand stroking her hair and shoulders while his lips nuzzled her neck. All but purring like a satisfied kitten, she cuddled against him. The only thing that marred her contentment was hunger. She hadn't eaten much lunch and was wishing for something now. But she didn't want to disturb Brandon by bringing up the subject.

However, the rumbling of her stomach finally made her condition obvious.

"Do I detect a protest at missing dinner?" Brandon murmured, a hint of laughter in his deep voice.

"I'm afraid so."

"Don't apologize. And then I won't have to apologize for the odd assortment of stuff that's in my refrigerator. Besides, I'm hungry, too."

He crossed to the closet and found a terry robe for himself, then looked back at Laura still huddled under the covers. "Making you get dressed doesn't seem fair. Want to wear something of mine?"

Nodding, she accepted a plaid flannel shirt and rolled up the sleeves. The tails hung well below her thighs, making the covering modest if not stylish.

He looked at her for a moment, taking in the picture she made with his oversized shirt and her dark locks slightly tangled from their lovemaking.

"I like it when you let your hair down," he whispered, using his fingers to comb her short, dark tresses from her forehead.

He couldn't see her flush in the semidarkness, but he caught the flash of her shy smile.

In the kitchen, they stood arm in arm before the refrigerator, inspecting the contents.

"I don't think we can split one leftover chicken leg," Brandon observed.

"No, but if you were a gentleman, you'd let me have it."

"Okay, I'm a gentleman."

She was already removing it, along with some fruit cocktail, two slices of pizza, and some cinnamon raisin buns.

"Now I know the kind of balanced diet you eat in secret," she observed.

He laughed and then sobered. "Actually, I tried a bunch of different things, but I didn't have much appetite this week."

"Me neither."

He squeezed her shoulder, and for a moment they were silent. It had been a long, lonely separation for both of them, and neither was inclined to mar the joy of this time together by talking about their estrangement yet.

"Let me put your chicken leg in the microwave," Brandon finally offered.

"You don't have to be that much of a gentleman. If we do the pizza first, you can have some too."

It took only a few minutes to get the impromptu meal together.

"Well, what kind of wine do you think goes with all this?" Brandon asked as he ceremoniously held out her chair.

"Wine? You've got to be kidding."

"No. This may not look like it, but it's a celebration. If I had champagne, I'd bring that out. But I'm afraid it's going to be more like *vin ordinaire*."

A bottle of rosé was the best compromise Brandon could come up with.

"To us," he proposed, handing her a stemmed goblet of the pale liquid.

"To us," she repeated, her blue eyes seeking his dark ones. All this was so new, so precious. It was hard to think further than this evening—let alone about the future.

They both found that they were ravenously hungry, yet it was impossible to concentrate only on the food. As they ate pizza and fruit cocktail and sipped their wine, they kept reaching out to twine their free hands together or touch each other on the arm. At the same time, Brandon's bare foot caressed her leg under the table. At first he confined himself to stroking her ankle and calf with his instep. But as the meal progressed, his toes began to walk themselves up her leg until they finally discovered the silky flesh of her inner thigh.

Laura grinned. "Just sharing a meal with you appears to be dangerous. Maybe I should ask for police protection."

Her words were light and teasing. But instead of responding in kind, Brandon stiffened and his brow furrowed.

"Damn! Laura, I'm sorry, I wasn't thinking at all— about protection. How could I have been so stupid? I could have gotten you pregnant tonight."

His words were like a sudden arctic wind swooping out of a frozen wasteland to turn her happiness to ice.

Why? she asked herself brokenly. Why now? It wasn't fair that the past was catching up with her so soon.

Pushing her chair back, she stood up.

"Laura, I'm sorry," he repeated, and then grinned as a new thought struck him. "But it's no tragedy. If you're pregnant, we'll just get married, that's all."

When he looked into her eyes, he knew something was terribly wrong. A moment ago there had been warmth and laughter sparkling in their blue depths. Now they had gone flat and dead.

"No we won't," she said, shaking her head slowly. The words were the hardest she had ever uttered, but once she started to speak, it was difficult to stop. "You don't have anything to worry about," she added with a frigid calm that masked the roiling turmoil of her emotions. "I can't get pregnant. I can't have any children."

For a long moment, neither of them spoke. Brandon reached out and tried to take her hand, hoping to reestablish the contact they had just been sharing. But she snatched it away and moved several feet farther from him until her back was pressed against the wall.

Brandon pushed his own chair away from the table and stood up quickly. In a few strides he reached her side and took her by the shoulders. "Laura, is that what's been troubling you all this time? Did you think that would make a difference to me?" he whispered.

"It did to someone else!" She couldn't see the naked pain that washed across her own features as she spoke, but there was something very close to it mirrored in Brandon's face. After all, he knew a lot about the anguish of loss himself.

"Do you want to tell me about it?" he questioned gently.

"No. But I will—so you'll know. That's only fair."

"Laura, that's not what I meant," he tried again. But he could see now that he wasn't reaching her. It was almost as though she were alone in the room, speaking for her own benefit.

Taking her hand, he led her to the sofa and sat her down gently before sinking onto the other cushion. But she didn't seem to be aware of her surroundings now.

"It wasn't because of anything I did," she began in a small voice, her eyes unseeing, her face bleak. "You know, just one of those things that happens. I was sick when I was fourteen. For a long time, they didn't know what it was because it's something—a kind of infection—girls that age don't usually get. But they knew what it did to me."

She paused and took a gulping breath. "When you're young, you don't realize the effect something like that is going to have on your life. Having kids, a family of your own, is just so far in the future."

Brandon's hands clenched at his sides. Laura looked so small and vulnerable sitting across from him. He wanted to pull her into his arms, to comfort her against the warmth of his body, to tell her that it was all right. But he had to let her finish.

"It wasn't until Arthur Henderson that I realized . . ." It was hard to get the words out now. But she forced herself to stumble on. "We were going to get married—until I told him. He said I should have let him know about it sooner. . . . He was from this family that traced their ancestors back to the *Mayflower* or something like that. I guess keeping the line going was really important to him. Or at least that's what he told me."

She started to talk about the letter Arthur had written her and about how that had made her feel, but Brandon didn't allow her to go on much more. Before she could move, he was across the sofa, pulling her against him, holding her with fierce intensity.

"Don't you understand?" he rasped. "None of that matters. I love you. I love *you*," he repeated.

"You don't have to say that," she whispered, her face hidden against his chest. For a moment, he clenched his teeth in frustration. Then, drawing back slightly, he tipped her chin up so that she was forced to meet his penetrating gaze.

"I do have to tell you. Because it's true," he insisted. "I love you—for yourself, for what our relationship gives me."

She stared at him uncomprehendingly. Never in her wildest imaginings could she have envisioned this scene or what he wanted her so desperately to understand.

Brandon saw that in her eyes, knew that she was simply incapable of adjusting her perception of reality so quickly. He understood now why she had built a wall around her emotions, why she had been unable to trust him, to give herself to him. She had been hurt too badly to dare open up so completely again. When she had asked him to make love to her earlier this evening, it had meant more than he ever could have realized.

Yet, he could still lose her if he couldn't make her understand the breadth and depth of his feelings for her. It was obvious that he couldn't reach her with mere words now, just as it had been that first night he'd kissed her. Then he had managed to break through to her on a much more basic level. His only hope was that he could do it again.

With vehement desperation, he lowered his lips toward hers. She tried to twist away, but he prevented her withdrawal. With one firm hand, he held her head, bidding her to accept the consuming mastery of his kiss. With all the persuasive skill at his command, he forced her lips apart, his tongue plunging deeply into the cavern of her mouth. He felt the stirrings of her response even as she tried to deny it. He wasn't going to let her lock her emotions away from him.

As his lips and tongue continued to tease and persuade, his hands stripped the oversize shirt from her slender body, uncovering it to his knowing, sensual touch once again. His fingers sought and stroked her. And when he felt her nipples harden in a response she was helpless to deny, he knew that he had won the first round.

"Brandon, no," she gasped, even as her body quivered and stirred under his touch.

"I told you once before, don't fight your feelings. Don't think," he murmured as his lips left hers to wander at random over her face, her shoulders, her breasts, nibbling and tantalizing as they went. "Just feel. Just feel what you mean to me, Laura, what we mean to each other."

His hands and lips were instruments of pleasure now, seeking and finding, demanding and bestowing everything that a man could give a woman—and asking nothing in return but her acknowledgment that they belonged together.

There was no way she could fight such a loving assault. She was his now, totally his. Her body arched to his touch like a slender reed bending to the wind; her nerve endings telegraphed a thousand sensual messages to her fevered brain.

This time when his name came to her lips, it was a plea of sweet urgency, not a protest.

She cried out again as the heat and hardness of his body merged with hers. She felt his shudder of gratification as she began, unbidden, to move with him. The joy of giving and taking was so intense that she felt as though she might be consumed by it. But it was only the prelude to the ultimate, exploding climax of sensation that they shared together.

"I love you." At the moment of supreme ecstasy, the words were on her lips—and on his, too.

She was conscious at first only of moisture upon her cheeks, and then realized that what she felt were her own tears. She had told Brandon the terrible secret she had walled up inside herself for so long, and he hadn't turned away. Instead, he had pulled her into his arms and made fiercely tender love to her. It was hard to believe that it was really true. But she couldn't deny what had just happened here on the couch in his living room.

Brandon looked down at her and gently touched one of the tiny rivulets, wiping it away with the side of his finger. "Don't cry," he whispered. "It's all right. It's going to be all right. I promise."

Her eyes were large and luminous in the darkness as he swung her up into his strong arms and carried her back to the warmth of his bed. Gently he helped her under the covers and then followed. He pulled her close, as though his body could protect her from the furies that had been following her for so long.

"I love you," she said again. "I was afraid of that before—of letting myself love."

"And now?"

"I'm still afraid—but not so much," she admitted.

She felt his strong arms clasp her shoulders. "That's a good start," he assured her. "A good start." And then the tension of the moment was broken as he chuckled. "You know, I hate to drag Franklin Roosevelt into bed with us, but what he had to say about fear was right."

Laura couldn't help smiling at the path his agile mind had taken. Roosevelt had said that "the only thing we have to fear is fear itself." Brandon wanted her to know that the same was true for her.

"Next you're going to tell me that politicians make

strange bedfellows," she murmured, surprised that her sense of humor had returned.

"No I'm not. I'm going to tell you to get some sleep now. It's been a long day for both of us. We can continue this discussion in the morning."

But long after she had fallen asleep in the safety of his arms, Brandon remained awake, staring thoughtfully into the darkness.

All the pieces of the puzzle that made up Laura Carson had finally fallen into place. At last he understood what she had lost and how she had been hurt—and why she had been so desperately afraid to open herself to his love.

Well, he had won an important battle tonight. And, as he had told Laura, that was a good start. But he knew there was still a war raging within the woman who slept so peacefully in his arms. And until the right side claimed victory, things could never really be settled between the two of them.

7

The feel of the bed shifting slightly woke Laura. For a moment, she was completely disoriented. But when Brandon moved gently against her body, her eyes snapped open.

"I'm sorry; I didn't mean to wake you," he murmured, smiling warmly over at her.

She could tell by the slight chill of his skin against her still sleep-warm body that he had been out of bed. And he confirmed her assumption moments later as he settled down more fully into the heated cave beneath the covers.

"I got out of here without waking you," he admitted, his arm encircling her shoulder. "But I guess I couldn't sneak back in."

It was a temptation to stay where she was, snug and secure in his arms—in his bed. But Laura sensed that the morning was already rather far advanced.

"I've got to call Sylvia and tell her I'll be late," she said drowsily, her eyes half-closed now that the first shock of orienting herself had worn off.

"No you don't. I've already taken care of that."

The words made Laura's eyes open fully. "What do you mean, already taken care of?"

"That's why I got up—to phone the garden center. I told Sylvia you came over for some early-morning landscape consulting."

"Consulting," Laura snorted, "you mean consorting."

Brandon couldn't repress a grin. "Now, you know I wouldn't tell her anything like that. Your dragon is perfectly capable of drawing her own conclusions. She said you should stay as long as you wanted—that she'd hold down the fort."

Laura felt her face redden. She wasn't used to spending the night in a man's bed—or sending out a general news bulletin on the fact the next morning. But Brandon remained unperturbed. "If you ask me, I think she likes the idea of our getting together almost as much as I do."

The matter-of-fact observation told Laura that he had made some rather sweeping assumptions about their relationship—assumptions that he hadn't bothered to discuss with her.

"Brandon," she began.

He sighed, catching the warning edge in her voice. "You're right, we have to get some things settled. That's why I called Sylvia. I don't want you to leave until we finish the discussion we started last night."

Brandon was already out of bed and crossing the oak floor toward the bathroom. "I'd suggest that we take a shower together, except that I know we'd never get any talking done afterward. Why don't you use the bathroom down the hall? There are towels in the linen closet next to it."

"All right," Laura agreed. Although they had just spent a very intimate night together, the idea of a shared shower was still a bit unsettling.

And so was the talk Brandon had proposed. The realization made her take as long as possible with her toilet. By the time she emerged from the bathroom dressed in the jeans and plaid shirt she had worn the day before, she could already smell the aroma of coffee perking.

As she made her way into the kitchen, Brandon turned away from the stove, where he was scrambling eggs.

"I was going to poke my head into the shower and ask you what you wanted, but I decided to forego the pleasure," he quipped.

"Eggs are fine," Laura assured him. "Is there anything I can do to help?" she added.

"You could pour the coffee."

She was glad for the activity. But when she and Brandon finally sat facing each other at the round oak table, she found her appetite had practically disappeared.

Brandon, too, was only sipping his coffee. "When it comes right down to it," he finally admitted, pushing his practically untouched plate away, "I think it's going to be talk first and eat later."

"All right, you seem to know what you want to discuss," Laura began with more resolve than she really felt.

Brandon nodded. "Do you like your life?" The query and the tone of his voice took her by surprise. Last night he had been comforting and reassuring. Now he was suddenly no longer making things easy.

"What kind of question is that?" she shot back.

"The most important one. Anyone who meets you can see that you're a successful businesswoman, a very creative person, a woman of wit and charm. But what about human contact, warmth, caring, closeness? How much of that has there been in your life over the past few years?"

Laura's face hardened. "I thought I made it clear last night—"

But Brandon didn't let her finish. "No. What you led me to believe last night was that you had found a way to make life safe—that at the age of twenty-seven you were through taking risks."

"I didn't want to get hurt again," she protested, pushing back her chair and standing up.

"You're so uptight, you can't even have a rational conversation about the subject," Brandon pointed out relentlessly. "But don't you dare try to run away from me again today. We're going to have this out."

Laura bit her lip. "Why are you doing this to me?" she asked.

"Not because I want to hurt you," he went on more gently. "But since I brought up the subject, let's explore the topic of getting hurt—and taking risks."

She waited warily for his words, sure that they would focus on her inadequacy. But his next remark was not what she had expected.

"You know," he continued, "after my wife and son were killed, I felt as though I didn't have anything to live for. For a long time, the only way I could cope with life was to cut myself off from it." He spoke almost matter-of-factly, as though he were discussing someone else. But Laura caught the emotion just under the surface of his words.

"That's why I could spend eighteen hours a day at Cornell working myself like a slave in that hotel management program," he continued. "I might as well have been a machine, not a man."

He paused for a moment, his expression thoughtful. "It was a long time before I could even imagine having a relationship with someone—loving someone—again. But I had begun to understand that the way I was living my life could hardly be called living. I had finally admitted to myself how much I missed warmth and caring and closeness. And then I met you.

"What is it," he went on, giving her a direct look, "that attracts one particular man to one particular woman? For me it was your voice, your sense of humor, your looks, your creativity, your sensitivity—even your vulnerability. But it was more than any of that, more than I can explain. It was as if someone had suddenly come in and thrown open the shutters in a tightly closed room. The light and heat were a revelation. But they were painful, too."

Laura felt her chest constrict, knowing how hard it was for him to open himself up like this. Brandon was describing exactly what she had felt when she first met him. Yet she hadn't been able to tell him about it.

He wasn't through talking. "You were obviously wary of involvement. I knew there was something very painful in your past. I guess I could recognize that from my own experience. And so I tried not to rush you into anything you weren't ready for. But that night after the auction, you were so warm and loving, I thought you had finally come to terms with our relationship, that you were ready to take the next step. So I let you know just how much I wanted you, how much I needed you, and you pushed me away."

The look of naked vulnerability on his face was almost too much for her to endure. But he wasn't going to turn away. "That hurt, you know. It hurt a lot. At first, I wasn't sure I wanted to try again. But after a few days of not seeing you, I knew I had to. When you came to the door yesterday afternoon, I thought you had come to the same conclusion."

"Oh, Brandon." The words were a strangled cry. It took a moment before she could continue, but his unburdening had made her own possible now. "I did want the same thing. I wanted you so badly that night, I ached. But I just couldn't let you make love to me." She swallowed hard, forcing herself to get the words out. "You see, with Arthur it was different. I don't think now that he ever really loved me. I think he was just looking for the right wife. He wasn't a very considerate lover. I never really enjoyed that part of our relationship. And I know this is going to sound crazy, but that was reassuring —even comforting."

Brandon's gaze remained fixed on her face. "What do you mean?"

"I mean, after what happened with Arthur, I knew I

wasn't like other women. I couldn't dare want the same things they did."

Brandon opened his mouth to speak, but Laura shook her head. "You had your say. Let me finish," she insisted. "I knew I was never going to marry. But I convinced myself it didn't matter—because I didn't respond to men, and I wasn't going to enjoy a sexual relationship anyway."

The troubled look in her eyes cleared. "And then you came along and changed all that—like a sorcerer waving a magic wand. The first night you kissed me, you made me realize why I hadn't responded to Arthur. You made me feel things I'd never felt, want things I'd never known existed. And I was so afraid of that."

"Laura." In an instant he had stood up, closed the gap between them, and pulled her out of her chair. Then he was folding her tightly into his arms. For a moment she clung to him, feeling that if she could just stay there, safe in the circle of his embrace, everything would be all right. But there were still things—critical things—that had to be said.

She lifted her head to search his face with troubled eyes. "Brandon, what you had before was obviously important to you, or the loss wouldn't have been so crushing. And I can't give you what you had then. I can't give you children."

"Yes," he admitted, reaching up to tenderly stroke her cheek, "my son was important to me. But he's gone. And you have to let me be the judge of what's important to me now. We only get one go-around in life, you know. Being with you has made me realize that I don't want to be half-alive anymore. I want to reach out and gather in every moment of living that I can. *And that means having you.*"

There was no argument she could muster to counter those words. And suddenly she knew she didn't want to. The look of love in his eyes was a caress, a plea, a promise.

It was time to stop talking and to start living. Her arms stole up his back to circle his neck. She pulled his head down to hers in a kiss that said more than mere words ever could. The freedom to revel in the mingling, moist pleasure of it was intoxicating. And this time, when Brandon began to move against her, she savored the knowledge that he was telling her yet again just what a desirable woman she was. The insight fueled her own need, and she trembled in his arms.

"Have you decided you don't want breakfast after all?" he teased huskily when he finally lifted his head.

"It's cold, anyway—and I'm hot," she added, almost but not quite shocked at her own brazen words.

Brandon chuckled. "That sounds like an invitation to return to bed, if I ever heard one."

Much later, he brought a tray of sandwiches ordered from Tony's Deli into the bedroom.

"This is a test, you understand," he informed her gravely. "If you get my bed full of crumbs, the rest of our meals will be at the dining room table."

"And if *you* get your bed full of crumbs?" she asked, attacking a roast beef sandwich with considerable appetite.

"Then you help me change the sheets."

"Not fair," she objected.

"Well, it's one of the house rules. And here's another one. If we have any problems, we bring them out into the open and talk about them. Okay?"

Laura nodded. He was right. Suddenly she was overwhelmed by a rush of tender feelings toward this man who had cared enough about her to force his way through the wall she had built around her emotions. "I love you, you know," she whispered, reaching out to press her hand over his. Just saying those words was like unlocking the gates to a rich kingdom she had always assumed she would never enter.

"I love you, too," he affirmed, moving over so that his shoulder touched hers.

For a while, they ate in silence. Then Brandon turned to her and grinned. "You know, while I was sulking, I was damned if I was going to call and ask. But I have been wondering when the deck and plantings are going to be finished."

"And now that you're sleeping with the landscape architect, you want to talk to her about business, too?" Laura inquired, matching his light tone.

"Precisely."

"Well, I was planning to send a crew out Monday morning to tackle the deck in earnest. Actually, I figured that if they showed up and started hammering at six-thirty, you might call me to complain."

"Thanks for the warning," Brandon grumbled good-naturedly.

"Not at all." Suddenly she looked over at him and smiled shyly. Was this really Laura Carson sitting in bed with a man, covered only by a sheet and bantering so intimately?

He smiled back, understanding her reaction. "It feels damn good, doesn't it?" he asked gruffly, giving her a quick hug.

"Yes."

And not only was it good, it kept on getting better and better. Laura realized that what she had experienced with Brandon up till now was just a taste of how things could be between a man and a woman who cared deeply about each other.

It wasn't just their lovemaking, which brought her to heights of joy she had never imagined existed. It was the warm, close, sharing relationship that kept unrolling like a bolt of brightly patterned fabric from a Christmas bazaar.

Of course, there *were* problems and conflicts. But Laura looked at the inevitable small frictions in their daily lives as a way of getting to know Brandon better. Even when he disagreed with her, it was obvious that he was willing to consider her side and that he wouldn't force her to go along with his point of view.

"All right, tell me again why you won't marry me next week?" he asked one evening as they carried bags of groceries into his kitchen. "Or why you won't at least move in here? You've got to admit," he grumbled as he stowed orange juice concentrate in the freezer, "that maintaining two households like this is inefficient."

"I know," Laura admitted, opening the pantry door and beginning to put away the canned goods. "But I'd feel funny living with someone I wasn't married to—even the man I love," she added quickly. "And marriage is just such a big step."

"For me too," Brandon reminded her.

Laura put away the last of the tomato sauce and stood up. Crossing the room, she came over to rest her head on his shoulder. "Brandon, I spent so many years telling myself I'd never share a home with anyone, that it's hard to adjust. I've got to have time to get used to the idea."

He stroked her cheek for a moment. "I know it's hard for you. And it's irrational of me, but that five percent uncertainty in you—I hope it's not more than five percent—still frightens me. I don't want there to be any chance of losing you. I want a contract, a piece of paper saying we belong to each other."

Laura nodded. "You're right. Most of me wants that too. In fact, sometimes I think I must be crazy turning down your proposals."

She angled herself away for a moment and gazed out the wide kitchen window, a faraway look in her eyes. She thought about the afternoon she'd helped Brandon unpack some boxes that he'd stored since before he'd left for Cornell. She was sitting at the desk in his office emptying one particularly dusty carton crammed with high school yearbooks, football programs and report cards. Laura was amused to find that Brandon had gotten a D in third-year French. She was just going to tease him about it when a square blue-bound album in the bottom of the box caught her eye. It didn't seem to fit in with the rest of the stuff.

When she opened it, she found out why. The cream-colored pages were full of pictures of a dark-haired baby boy who looked a lot like Brandon. In fact, Brandon was actually featured in a number of the photos—giving the baby a bottle or a bath or simply playing with him. In some of the pictures he was grinning. In some his face held such a look of tender love that her heart gave a lurch inside her chest.

He noticed she was absorbed in something and came over to stand behind her, watching her turn the pages for a moment. When she felt his presence, she looked up at him.

"Jason?" she questioned in a shaky voice.

"Yes." He reached out to smooth his finger across one of the pictures.

"You loved him very much, didn't you?"

"Yes, Laura, I did." His own voice was prickly with emotion. "And I want to be able to remember him. That's why I've saved this album. Some day I'll be able to look through it without feeling sad. But not yet."

"Are you sure . . ." she murmured, unable to finish the question. But he knew she was asking about his future, not his past.

Reaching down, he snapped the album closed. He pulled her to her feet, wrapped his arms around her and held her close. "Laura, those pictures are from another life. And I can't bring it back. But we're the future," he whispered fiercely. "Do you understand that?"

She hesitated for a moment.

"Do you?" he repeated.

"Yes." She had uttered the word because she loved him and because it was what she knew he wanted to hear—needed to hear—at the time.

That had been weeks ago. But sometimes the scene still popped into her thoughts. If she could only be certain that he would be content with their future. But how was she to be sure?

"You look so far away. What are you thinking?" he asked now, putting his hand on her shoulder.

She turned to him and smiled. "That I love you."

"I love you, too. And to prove it, I'll stop trying to pressure you. How about a glass of wine instead?"

Laura smiled, glad to escape her doubts and uncertainties. "You mean you'd rather ply me with strong drink?" she asked.

It was a private joke she'd repeated often since the evening he'd brought home a bottle of champagne to share. That particular day had been a tiring one for Laura, and after downing two glasses, she'd fallen asleep on the sofa while Brandon prepared dinner.

"Fat lot of good plying you with strong drink would do me," he reminded her.

"Touché."

Although Brandon liked to tease Laura about that one lapse, sharing some white wine in the evening and talking over their respective days together had become one of their most comfortable habits.

After bringing their glasses out to the just-completed deck and settling into padded lounge chairs, they sat for a few moments without speaking, sipping the clear, fruity liquid and enjoying the breathtaking setting. Finally, Brandon turned to Laura. "You know that the conference center zoning case is coming up in a few weeks?"

"Yes. I got another call from Tim Warfield asking if I wanted to come to a meeting of business people interested in discussing the problems the project might cause."

"I hope you told him what he could do with his meeting."

Since Laura had come to Brandon with the preliminary report, he'd dug out his draft of the final recommendations. It was apparent from reading it that General

Development was willing to go to considerable lengths to make the conference center an asset, not a liability, to the community. But Laura knew that there were plenty of well-meaning people like Tim who still thought the project would create more problems than it would solve.

Now she hesitated for a moment, taking a small sip of her wine. "Actually, I think I should go."

Brandon raised a questioning eyebrow.

"Think about it," Laura urged. "In the first place, I can let you know what they're planning. But I have more than just playing Mata Hari in mind. I think that if I can give those people the real story, a lot of the opposition will evaporate."

Brandon turned his glass in his hand, considering her argument. "You do have a point," he finally conceded. "But I can't help feeling as if I'm sending you into a lion's den."

"You're not *sending* me. I'm volunteering," Laura pointed out.

Brandon nodded thoughtfully. "I guess you're right. In fact, to avoid any conflict of interest, you're going to have to plan what you say to them without any coaching from me." He paused and gave her a direct look. "But they may try to nail you for that, anyway. Can you take the heat if someone tries to make it look as if you're on my side because we're all but living together?"

"I hadn't thought of that angle," Laura admitted, her brow wrinkling. "Tim would never stoop to a tactic like that. But if Kramer brings it up, I'll just point out that he's obscuring the issue. After all, the revised General Development report is on file with the Zoning Commission now. And it should speak for itself."

"If anyone can carry that off, you can," Brandon approved. He paused again, considering his words carefully and setting his empty glass down on the table between them before starting to speak. "You know, after you brought me that bootlegged report, my company started doing some investigating into how it got out. Kramer apparently paid for it."

Laura looked disgusted. "I guess I didn't think even he would stoop to something like that."

"Well, he has a lot to lose if we get approval," Brandon continued. "We've also gotten wind of some downtown hotel deal of his own, which he was cooking up before we came along."

Laura's eyes widened. "You mean he's opposed to you because he really wants to do something similar himself?"

"We think so, but he's been careful about it. There's no concrete proof. I'm just telling you to strengthen your resolve in case he starts fighting dirty."

"I never trusted him," Laura admitted, setting her own empty glass down beside Brandon's. "Now I know why."

"Probably a lot of other people don't either. And that will be to your advantage. Just remember, you were a respected businesswoman in Harperstown long before you got mixed up with the likes of me. That will count with people like Tim."

Laura grinned. "I like being mixed up with the likes of you. And I'm glad you think I can make a difference."

"I hope you can. If this turns into a long-drawn-out fight, it's going to be expensive. And it could generate a lot of bad feelings. In fact, that's actually how this whole conversation got started in the first place," Brandon explained. "My boss is very concerned about how this thing is handled, so he's asked me to come back to Chicago for some strategy meetings."

Laura forced her voice to sound light. "Our first separation—except for that stupid week when we weren't talking to each other. How long are you going to be gone?"

"Unfortunately, it looks like ten days. Henry decided that if I was coming back, he might as well schedule appointments with everyone who's wanted to see me since I came out here."

"Ten days," Laura repeated, suddenly realizing just how long that was going to be.

"You know I wouldn't go if I didn't think it was important."

"Yes, I know."

A week without Brandon only showed Laura how much he had become a part of her life. It wasn't that she couldn't keep occupied. Business at the garden center was now bustling. There were a number of important design commissions to engage her creative energies. And Laura started planning her strategy for the confrontation with Kramer's group, using her own notes and the revised report that Brandon had left her, along with actual blueprints for the project. But there was still a large gap in her life that couldn't really be filled by late-night phone calls from Chicago.

In order to hold her loneliness at bay, Laura began to make plans for Brandon's homecoming. He had told her he would be flying in to Baltimore late Wednesday afternoon. And that would mean he'd be home in time for dinner. The first meal after their separation was going to be very special—and very elegant, she decided. She'd make teriyaki steak to commemorate their first dinner together. And she'd round out the meal with rice pilaf, broccoli with hollandaise sauce, and cherry cheesecake. They'd eat inside, with candles and flowers on the table, and she'd bring over the good china she usually kept stowed away in the top of her kitchen cabinets.

Over the weekend, she visited Harperstown's most exclusive dress shop and found the perfect dress for the occasion. It was a long, emerald green jersey creation that hugged her figure suggestively—the kind of thing she would only feel comfortable wearing for a private tête-à-tête. Silver slippers, silver earrings and a stunning necklace of heavy silver beads that her mother had sent from New Mexico would complete the ensemble.

While she was dress-shopping, workmen were busy solving the only remaining problem, the view, which she wanted to be as perfect as the rest of the setting. Although the deck was completed, spring rains had kept her landscaping team off the steep slope. In fact, after the construction crew had finished dragging their equipment around the back of the house and removing it again, the grounds looked worse than when she had made that first sketch of the property.

"I'd like to have Brandon's landscaping completed before he gets back," she had told Sylvia on Thursday morning. "I'm thinking of taking some men off of other projects so we can get the terracing done over the weekend—because until that's finished, we can't go ahead with the rest of the planting."

"That's going to mean putting some other jobs behind schedule. But if that's what you want to do . . ."

"It's what I want to do."

Sylvia put down the loose-leaf scheduling book and grinned. "If Brandon McGuire were anyone else, you'd be charging him ten percent extra for the inconvenience. But he's not even going to know he got special treatment, is he?"

"Can't you ever let me have any fun?" Laura complained. "My reward is going to be the pleased astonishment on his face when he walks out on the deck and sees the whole project finished."

Sylvia gave her a fond look. "Actually, I've been watching you have fun ever since that man arrived on the scene. I've never seen you look so happy and so content. I've enjoyed getting to know Brandon. He's really some kind of guy!"

"Thanks for making it possible for me to spend so much time with him," Laura returned.

"As I said, it's my pleasure. Besides, I know it's not *just* fun. Even watching from the sidelines, I can see the two of you have something very special going."

"Yes," Laura agreed. "And I'm finally getting used to it. The next time he asks me to marry him, I think I'm going to say yes."

Sylvia stared at Laura in disbelief. "You mean that gorgeous, sexy, attentive man has asked you to marry him and you've turned him down?"

Laura nodded. "Sylvia, you and I have worked together and we've been good friends. But there was something about myself that I could never talk about—not even to you. I've known for a long time that I can't have children."

"Oh, Laura . . ."

But the younger woman shook her head. "The truth is that, until I met Brandon, I let that one fact rule my whole life. I told myself that I could never have a normal relationship with a man—that I could never marry. But Brandon wouldn't accept that. He convinced me that it doesn't matter to him. But he did something else for me, too, something that I don't think I realized until just now. He forced me to face my fears. And bringing the whole thing out into the open has made a tremendous difference to me. I don't know how to describe it, but it's as if this horrible weight has been lifted off my chest, and now, after all these years, I can finally breathe properly. I mean, once I had talked about it with him and the world didn't come to an end, I knew I didn't have to keep it hidden from everybody else anymore."

"I'm glad. You know, Laura, I realized there was something troubling you," Sylvia conceded. "But you were so self-sufficient. You wouldn't let anybody get really close."

The younger woman nodded. "I know. But I couldn't help it."

"And I could never come out and ask what was

making a beautiful, smart, creative woman like you act as though deep down she thought she wasn't worth anything." Sylvia stood up. "But that's all in the past now."

"Yes. And for the first time in years, I feel as if I really have a future that I can look forward to."

8

The immediate future, however, didn't go quite as Laura had planned. One of her landscaping and construction crews was able to finish terracing Brandon's steep hill and start putting in the plants she had selected. By Wednesday, it looked as though everything was going to be in place before his return—until several of her other workmen called in sick. Since they were part of the crew rushing to landscape a model home park before the grand opening, and that job had top priority, Laura was forced to replace them with the men who had been working on Brandon's home.

"I can't let that developer down," she told Sylvia with a sigh. "He's been a good customer. And besides, our contract specifies that we have to finish on time—or pay a penalty."

The older woman nodded sympathetically as she arranged vegetable seed packets in the rack by the check-out counter. "I know you wanted everything to be perfect for Brandon this evening, but I'm sure he'll understand."

Laura glanced at her watch. "It's only ten-thirty, and he won't be home till dinnertime. If you can spare me here, I'll go over and finish the job myself."

"Yourself?" Sylvia said in surprise. "That's pretty heavy work, you know."

"I know. But I've done it before," Laura replied. "Besides, I had my heart set on getting things ready before Brandon came home."

"Well, at least have one of the guys help you load the truck," Sylvia suggested. "On second thought, why don't you have somebody drive you out there and help with the unloading, too? Brandon can give you a ride home later."

Laura nibbled thoughtfully on her lip as she considered the proposal. "Since I've already stashed the groceries and the dress I'm going to wear this evening at his house, that's a good idea," she agreed.

Forty-five minutes later, she and Gary turned into the steep drive that led to Brandon's house.

As she pulled on a pair of heavy gardening gloves, Laura paused for a moment to admire the effect she had created at the front of Brandon's property.

White dogwoods and delicate pink azaleas flanked the parking area. Low, graceful cottoneaster bushes lined the flagstone walk, and taller rhododendrons were grouped in several artful clusters. Here and there, impatiens in shades of pink would provide color throughout the summer.

It took another twenty minutes for Laura and Gary to carry more azaleas, peat moss and mulch down the newly constructed stairway along the side of Brandon's house.

"Are you sure you don't want me to stay?" the young man offered.

"No. Sylvia needs you," Laura told him, tying a red bandanna around her hair to keep it out of her eyes. As

Gary turned to leave, she began setting out the flowering bushes along the terraced hill. They were in various hues of pink and red ranging from a very intense raspberry to a delicate shade called strawberry ice. Many landscapers would have been too timid to use such combinations together, but Laura was an expert in creating striking effects with the subtle interplay of shades.

Before doing any planting, Laura moved the bushes around, paying close attention to the contrast of colors. Rather than line the shrubs up along the terraces, she clustered them in groups for a natural effect against the steep hillside.

When she was finally satisfied, she began to dig the necessary holes on one of the terraces. Luckily the ground was soft from all the excavation or it would have been a much harder job. Next she filled each hollow halfway with peat moss and mixed it with top soil before setting in the bushes and packing down the dirt around the roots. Each plant would need a good watering. But that was a messy job, and she'd take care of it when she finished everything else.

After completing one level, she stood back to catch her breath and survey her handiwork with satisfaction. The terrace looked good. But she wished she could say the same for her clothing. Clumps of mud clung to her tennis shoes and streaked her jeans. And only the bandanna around her head kept small rivulets of perspiration from running down her face. The day was hotter and the work a bit harder than she'd anticipated.

Laura glanced at her watch. At least there was going to be plenty of time to get cleaned up before Brandon's arrival. As soon as she planted the last of the bushes, she'd shower, wash her hair and change into a clean shirt and jeans. She wouldn't put on her new dress until dinnertime. Luckily she had several changes of casual clothes in Brandon's closet and even a cache of underwear in his bureau.

Unconsciously smiling to herself, she picked up her

shovel and walked down to the next terrace. It was funny, she mused, how easily she had accommodated herself to living part time in his home. But Brandon did have a point. It would be a lot easier if they were maintaining only one household.

Most of the morning, Laura had forced herself to focus on the landscaping and not Brandon. But now that he had intruded upon her thoughts, it was impossible to prevent her attention from returning to him as she dug holes and mixed peat moss with top soil. He would be wearing a suit or a sport jacket this evening and not his usual jeans, she mused, remembering how a jacket emphasized his broad shoulders. She went on from there to imagine how it would feel to be enfolded in his strong arms. The wayward thoughts made her suddenly ache for that close, intimate contact. She could almost smell the after-shave he used, and under it the special scent of his clean skin.

She shivered slightly as she played back a mental recording of his voice, hearing the rich-rough texture that had first attracted her over the phone. And when she closed her eyes for a moment, she found herself picturing the masculine planes of his face and the dark eyes that could change so quickly from laughing to passionate. She could almost feel the intensity of his gaze burning into the back of her neck.

The prickling sensation was so vivid that she whirled around and looked up at the lower level of the wide deck that now graced the back of the house.

There, leaning comfortably against the wooden guard rail, was Brandon himself, dressed in black slacks and the tweed sport coat she had been imagining. Laura's jaw dropped open in disbelief.

"Hi," he greeted her as though he'd just been down to the corner store to buy a quart of milk. And yet the huskiness in his voice and the intensity of his eyes belied his casual salute. As he took in the details of her face and body, she knew what it was to be devoured with a look.

In truth, she was doing the same thing, her gaze taking over from her imagination to catalog Brandon's attractions. He was just as handsome, just as compelling as she had imagined. She must have known subconsciously he was there, she reasoned, a private smile flickering at the corners of her mouth.

"I was thinking about you," she said wonderingly.

"I was thinking about you, too. That's why I finished up my business last night and took an early plane home this morning."

The words broke Laura's trance, and her gloved hand flew to the bandanna that held back her hair. "My God, Brandon, I didn't expect you so early. I look like a gypsy—a very dirty gypsy."

"Maybe like a gypsy," he conceded, "but a very lovely one."

"You can't mean that." She looked down at her mud-caked shoes and streaked jeans.

"What exactly are you doing down there?" Brandon questioned.

Laura groaned. "I had this perfect little dinner planned. And I wanted the landscaping to look perfect too. So I was finishing it up because half my workmen are sick and there was no one to help."

Brandon took in her obvious distress. "Since I seem to have wrecked your plans, I'll help get the job finished—if you tell me what to do," he offered, stripping off his tweed jacket and laying it over the railing. Before Laura could stop him, he came down the wooden stairs and then stepped off onto the hill. Immediately the rich black shine of his polished shoes was covered by muddy soil.

"Brandon, you can't come down here; you'll get as dirty as I am," Laura protested.

"I'm already down here. And if I don't care about my shoes, why should you?"

As he spoke, he closed the distance between them with a few long strides. "I missed you, Laura," he growled. Before she could answer, he was encircling her with his arms. The embrace was as she had imagined, except that the reality of the close contact with his warm body was even more vivid than her anticipation.

"Oh, Brandon," she breathed. "I missed you, too. I missed you so much."

"So much," he echoed, his voice a rough caress. For that moment in time, she forgot all about the landscape project, the mud, her disheveled appearance. There was only the reality of Brandon McGuire filling her senses, making her realize what it was to be fully alive—and in love.

When he drew back slightly, his eyes were glowing coals. And yet a smile curved his lips. "I do intend to help with those bushes," he murmured. "But first . . ."

Mesmerized, she watched as his hands went to the front of her shirt and began slowly to undo the buttons.

"Brandon . . ." she began, but further words became impossible as he dispatched the last of the buttons and pushed the edges of her shirt back so that the cups of her ecru lace bra were exposed.

"I'm sure gypsies don't have such sexy underwear," he whispered, his hands stroking the all-but-transparent fabric.

A little gasp of pleasure escaped Laura's lips. Her breasts seemed to lift and swell toward Brandon, and at the same time, her nipples hardened.

"God, I missed you," he repeated. This time the words were a ragged groan as he bent so that his lips could find those straining peaks through the wispy fabric. Laura's back arched, and her arms went to his neck to steady her trembling body.

It was already impossible to stand without clinging to him. And when his hand slid up the inside of her thigh to the juncture of her legs, she felt the world begin to spin crazily. His fingers cupped around her femininity, pressing and stroking through the denim fabric, creating sensations that made her breath catch in her throat.

"Do you remember that time out here on the patio when I brushed the mulch off your bottom? Well, it was a wonderful excuse to touch you. But I wanted to do this, too."

"But that was before . . ." she managed.

"Not before I wanted you."

For a moment, his hand pressed her even more tightly, then reluctantly withdrew.

Laura's heavy-lidded eyes opened. She heard his ragged breathing, her own.

Brandon, leaning back against one of the supporting posts of the deck, took a deep, steadying breath. Then, very carefully, he reached out and began rebuttoning the front of her shirt.

"What are you doing?"

"Getting ready to plant those bushes."

"You can't mean it. Not now. Not when . . ."

He grinned. "Oh, but I do. It's the least I can do to make up for spoiling your surprise. And just think how glad we're both going to be when the job is finished."

"Are you some sort of sadist?"

"A masochist, I think. But you did feel it was important to get that planting done before dinner, didn't you?"

Laura sighed. Yes, she had wanted to get the planting finished, but somehow that objective had gotten lost when Brandon had started unbuttoning her shirt. However, if he thought he could calmly go to work now, then so could she.

"All right," she agreed, "let's get to it. Do you see those bushes sitting down on the next terrace? Well, move each of them to the side and dig a hole for it that's a little deeper than the root ball."

Brandon snapped to attention. "Yes, ma'am."

For fifteen minutes he dug new holes while she packed the dirt around the azaleas she had just planted. Then she helped him mix peat moss with top soil and they planted the remaining bushes.

"It looks great," he complimented, stepping back to survey her colorful arrangement. "Are we finished now?" he added hopefully.

"No, the soil still has to be packed down around the roots, and then I've got to water the whole hill. Why don't you press down the soil while I get the hose?"

Laura disappeared around the corner, where she turned on the water. When she returned, Brandon was hunkered down by one of the bushes, tamping soil around the roots as she had directed. He had stood up and was about to move on to the next bush, when he changed his mind and leaned over to make some further adjustment.

Somehow the unguarded pose gave her a wicked idea—one that was hard to resist. Without giving herself time to consider the consequences of her actions, Laura adjusted the nozzle of the hose to a narrow flow and aimed the stream of water at Brandon's posterior. It hit squarely in the center of his dark slacks. It was the sort of thing she and her friends might have done to each other as kids on a hot day like this. But Brandon certainly wasn't prepared for the playful turn her mind had taken.

Yelping in surprise as the cold water soaked through to his flesh, Brandon straightened up and whirled around so that the water hit the front of his pants as well. It took him a moment to realize what had happened. And when he did, Laura knew that she had made a serious error in judgment.

"So you want to play dirty, do you?" he said, taking a step toward her. The half-angry, half-wicked expression on his face told Laura her little joke had backfired.

"No, I'm sorry. It was a mistake," she protested. But she ended up spoiling the apology with a giggle.

Brandon's answering grin let her know she was definitely in trouble. She backed up, quickly but she wasn't fast enough. It took Brandon only a few steps to close the distance between them.

"A mistake all right," he agreed, lifting the hose from

her hands and turning it around so that the cold stream of water shot down the front of her blouse.

Laura gasped as the icy liquid connected with her sun-warmed flesh. Then some instinct for self-preservation took over. Grabbing the hose, she tried to wrest it from Brandon's grasp.

"Oh, no, you don't," he grunted as they struggled.

Water seemed to be hitting her everywhere. And, while it was drenching him too, there was no way she could win this contest, Laura realized. "All right. Uncle. Uncle," she gasped. Brandon gave her a satisfied look and twisted the nozzle to "off" before tossing it aside. But before Laura could breathe a sigh of relief, he had grabbed her wrists.

"You need to be taught a lesson, young lady," he growled with mock ferocity, forcing her to her knees in front of him. She was so surprised that, before she knew it, he had pulled her down to the now-muddy ground and thrown his body on top of hers.

"What are you doing?" she gasped.

"You'll find out."

Pride made her keep struggling. But it soon became obvious that she was only fighting a weak delaying action. In less than a minute, Brandon had easily flattened her in the wet dirt, pulled her arms to her sides, and then clamped them in place with his knees. The way he straddled her body made it apparent that there was absolutely no chance of getting away.

His arms were free, and, for a moment he looked into her eyes and grinned again—this time with satisfaction. Then, slowly, he reached down and began to move his fingers against her rib cage and up into her armpits.

It tickled.

"Oh, no, Brandon, don't," she gasped between what quickly became hysterical giggles. But he only continued to grin down at her while he kept up the maddening titillation.

She writhed under him, almost as though she were in pain.

"Oh, please stop. Please!" she gasped.

"Do you promise never to pull that juvenile trick again?" he demanded.

"Yes."

"And do you admit you deserve your punishment?"

"Yes."

"And have you learned your lesson?" For emphasis, he gave her ribs another mock caress with his fingers.

"Yes," she managed when she could speak again.

"Good." Shifting his weight, Brandon allowed her to move her arms.

Laura drew in a deep breath.

He shook his head. "I knew you had a warped sense of humor, but that really was going a bit too far."

"I know." Reaching up, she brushed at a streak of dirt on his cheek. "You're a mess," she informed him.

He inspected her face and clothing. "So are you."

They both laughed. And then, as his ebony gaze captured her blue one, his expression changed—and so did hers. It was as though they had both suddenly become aware that he was straddling her hips, his body pressed intimately against hers.

"Laura."

He might have intended to stand up and help her to her feet. Instead, he shifted his position so that he was lying on top of her again. Before they had been struggling in mock battle. Now there was no thought in either of their minds except to touch, to feel, to savor the other.

"God, I want you," he groaned, his arms circling her shoulders, his leg parting hers so that he could lie between them. He moved urgently against her, frustrated by the barrier of clothing that separated them.

"Yes." His body moved against hers like flint on steel, igniting fires that only he could put out. She felt the same frustration that he did.

She heard his ragged breathing—or was it her own?

"How did we get ourselves into this very literal mess?" he rasped.

"I believe you were teaching me a lesson."

"Remind me next time I get the notion that I'd rather be in bed—and I don't mean a flower bed."

Reluctantly levering himself off her, Brandon stood up and held out his hand to help her rise.

"I'd offer to brush the dirt off your back," he muttered thickly, "but I think it's hopeless this time."

"What do you suggest—I mean, if you don't want me to leave clumps of mud all over your house?"

"I suggest that you go inside and get undressed. Leave your clothes and shoes right by the back door. Then you can go upstairs and take a shower. I'll take one in the bathroom on this level."

Laura's eyes widened. "Let me get this straight. You mean you want me to take off my clothes in the basement and walk upstairs naked?"

"Exactly. But don't worry, I won't peek. I don't think I could take it, seeing your breasts, the curve of your hips, that gorgeous dark triangle."

Laura's breath caught in her throat. It was as though he had touched each of those places instead of simply naming them. Before he could say anything else, she scurried inside and closed the door firmly behind her.

It took her longer than she expected to get out of her ruined clothing. The wet buttonholes were hard to work. When she was finally naked and standing beside a little heap of soggy clothes on the cement floor, several minutes had passed.

Laura had just crossed the basement and was about to put her foot on the first riser of the stairs when she heard the door open. Whirling, she saw Brandon across the room. Their eyes locked for an instant before she felt his smoldering gaze on her totally exposed body. It was one thing to be naked in Brandon's bed. It was quite another to meet him unexpectedly like this.

"You're not supposed to be here," he breathed, taking a step toward her.

"I wasn't going to be. But the buttons . . ." The rest of the explanation was swept away by the heat of his gaze.

She stood frozen there for another moment like a frightened deer caught unexpectedly in the headlights of a car. And then she turned and dashed up the stairs.

Entering Brandon's guest bathroom, Laura paused to take a look at herself in the mirror and groaned. Her arms and face were streaked with mud and her hair was plastered to her head. Moreover she was covered with goose bumps—as much from her cold dash upstairs as from Brandon's scorching look.

It took only a few minutes under the warm shower spray to make her feel better. Closing her eyes, she tilted her head back and let the water course through her hair while she soaped and rinsed her body. Then she opened a bottle of strawberry-scented shampoo she had left behind on one of her previous visits and worked up a rich lather.

She had just rinsed her hair for the second time and turned off the water, when she felt a momentary gust of cold air and knew that the bathroom door had been opened and closed.

"Brandon?"

"You were expecting someone else?"

Laura giggled. "Actually, no."

"Good." As he spoke, Brandon threw open the shower door.

Laura couldn't see much of him because he was holding a large white towel in his outstretched arms. But his shoulders, legs and arms were naked. "Come on out and let me dry you off," he offered.

Stepping forward, Laura found herself enfolded in white terry cloth—and Brandon's muscular arms.

"Mmmm, you smell like strawberries," he murmured, the heat of his breath on her cheek. Folding her close, he began to rub and pat her back and shoulders dry. Feeling slightly limp from the warm water, Laura let him minister to her, leaning her head down with an unconsciously sensual motion so that he could rub her hair.

But as he began to move the heavy fabric across her breasts and down her front, her senses came fully awake.

She hadn't realized a towel could be an erotic instrument. But then, there were lots of things she hadn't realized until she'd gotten to know Brandon McGuire.

She sighed as his terry-covered hand slid up her leg to the velvety skin of her inner thigh and then began to dry the dark triangle he had spoken of earlier. Her body had a flushed glow now—and not just from the heat of the shower.

When Brandon let the fabric slide away from his fingers so he could touch her still more intimately, she couldn't suppress a little gasp.

"Laura, it's been so long," he groaned, dropping the towel to the floor so that his hands could drift over her quivering flesh.

She knew now what she had only suspected before— that he was naked like herself and fully aroused. In the steamy light of the bathroom, she could see that his body was as flushed as hers and taut with desire for her.

A current of hot intensity seemed to flow between them now, drawing their fevered bodies together and at the same time robbing Laura of the ability to stand. She swayed against Brandon, clung to him, felt herself lifted up and carried to the bedroom.

He didn't need to ask if she was ready. Her body told him. And so did the little entreaties that tumbled from her lips. He was inside her almost before he had laid her on the crisp sheets, moving with a fierce urgency that drove them toward climax. It was only moments before she cried out her ecstasy, and then he did too.

9

I love you."

"I love you."

They clung together, savoring the aftermath of their passion.

"That was spectacular."

"Mmm . . ."

Brandon reached down and pulled the covers up around their shoulders and then nuzzled his face against Laura's breasts. "I can't tell you how good it is to be home," he murmured.

"And to have you back." As she spoke, she ran her fingers possessively through his thick dark hair.

"Will you marry me?" he asked huskily.

"Yes."

Brandon looked up, his gaze seeking hers. "Why?"

Laura's blue eyes were impish as she stared back at him. "Now that's a wonderful comeback. You ask a woman to marry you, and when she says yes, you ask why?"

"But when you've already asked her and been turned down half a dozen times, the question about her motives is a bit more natural."

"Granted." Laura took a deep breath. "I guess I've finally admitted to myself that I love you too much to let you get away." As if to emphasize the point, she reached out to tangle her fingers in the thick hair that spread across his broad chest.

Brandon gathered her against himself, pressing her close. "You mean being separated from me for almost two weeks did the trick?" As he spoke, his lips nuzzled the top of her dark head.

"Yes."

She heard him chuckle. "You know, I thought it might. That's why I arranged to be away for so long. Only, as usual, my ploy backfired. I finally couldn't stand it any more. So I came home early."

"You devil!" Laura pushed herself away from him, her blue eyes glittering like reflective glass. "You mean there were no meetings in Chicago?"

"Oh, there were meetings, all right. I just set up a bunch of extra appointments." He studied her fierce expression, his own a study in contrition. "Don't be angry. It did work out, after all."

Laura shook her head. "A typical male trick," she muttered under her breath. But when he pulled her back to his side, she didn't resist. He stroked her shoulders and then reached up to comb his fingers lovingly through the thick mass of her hair.

"And now that one shock is out of the way," he finally said, "I have another—although I hope it won't be quite so traumatic."

"Yes?"

"When I was back home, I couldn't stop talking about you. And one of the people I blabbed to was my mother. She wouldn't let me rest until I promised that she could meet you."

Laura leaned back and closed her eyes. "Do you think I'll pass muster?" she asked in a small voice.

Brandon reached down to weave his fingers with hers reassuringly. "This isn't one of my tests. You don't have to pass muster with anyone. But even if you did, you wouldn't have a thing to worry about." He paused and chuckled. "I've stacked the deck in your favor—to mix our metaphors again. Mom already knows how beautiful you are, how talented, that you're a good cook, that you have an—ahem—great sense of humor, that you know your way around an antique auction and a lot more things. But most important of all, she knows that I love you very much."

"Well, that's quite an advance notice," Laura conceded. "But could anyone possibly live up to it?"

"I told you. You already have."

"And when will your mother be here?"

"Day after tomorrow. I thought you might want some time to get your blouses and jeans out of my closet—and your bras and panties out of my dresser drawers. Not that I mind. But you know how mothers are."

"How considerate of you. I guess I'm just lucky she wasn't standing up there on the balcony with you this morning."

Brandon grinned. "No way. I wanted our reunion to be strictly private. And by the way, I do have one more confession to make."

"It figures," Laura interjected.

"I called Sylvia from the airport to find out where you'd be. She told me—quite gleefully, I might add—that you were here alone. That's why you didn't hear my car. I parked down at the end of the driveway."

"Remind me to strangle her."

"Oh, no. She did us a favor. She had planned to send Gary back here to find out how you were getting along by yourself. I told her not to."

"Sometimes I think we might as well just rent a billboard announcing that we're having an affair."

"Not anymore. It's an engagement." As he spoke, Brandon gently removed his arm from her shoulders and swung his legs out of bed. "I was pretty confident about my strategy," he remarked as he crossed the room and opened a dresser drawer.

When he turned around, he was holding a small velvet box.

"For you," he offered huskily, holding out his hand.

Laura sat up, pulling the sheet around her breasts. Almost afraid to breathe, she opened the lid. Inside, nestled in more dark velvet, was a sparkling diamond solitaire ring.

"Oh . . ." was all she could manage.

Brandon sat down on the side of the bed.

"Do you like it?" he questioned, looking anxiously down at her.

"Like it! Oh, Brandon, it's beautiful."

He sighed with relief. "Then try it on," he urged.

Laura lifted the ring out of the box and slipped it on the third finger of her left hand. It was a perfect fit. For a moment she looked down at the brightly sparkling gem set in a simple white gold band, seeing it not just for its beauty but also for what it symbolized. When her eyes lifted to Brandon's, they were misty.

Leaning over, he kissed her on the cheek, thought better of the chaste gesture, and found her lips with his. It was a long moment before either of them spoke.

"I love you," he affirmed again.

"Oh, and how I love you," she sighed, resting her head against his strong shoulder. But in the next moment, she couldn't suppress a grin as she looked down at his still-unclothed body beside her on the bed. "I don't suppose you're going to describe this particular nude scene to your mother when you tell her about our engagement."

He grinned back. "No. I believe I'll let her think that I proposed at dinner."

"Well, I won't tell if you won't."

Brandon grinned again as he lay back down beside her on the bed. But Laura could see the lines of fatigue in his face.

"Tired?"

"Yes. My schedule in Chicago really *was* hectic. And I had to get up at an ungodly hour to catch that plane."

Laura glanced at her watch. Though the drawn shades had dimmed the light in the room, it was still early in the afternoon.

"Want to take a nap?"

"Um-hum." He snuggled into her warmth. "And when I wake up, I want . . ."

"To have that dinner I promised you," she finished for him.

"That too."

It was much later that Laura finally changed into the elegant emerald green dress she'd bought for Brandon's homecoming, and donned the silver jewelry and slippers that she'd chosen to accent it.

Since she'd worked so hard in the morning, he had insisted on cooking the dinner while she dressed.

When she stepped out onto the deck, he lifted his gaze from the grill where the teriyaki steak sizzled aromatically.

"Beautiful," he murmured. "You almost make me wish I'd come home at the proper time."

Feeling regal and sexy, she smiled and pirouetted for him. "You mean you like me better this way than as a grubby gypsy girl?"

He pretended to consider the question. "Well, *she* was good in the bushes. And good in bed, too."

"Brandon!" Just when she thought she had learned to cope with his intimate banter, he came out with something more outrageous.

He studied the clinging lines of the dress, which emphasized her slender curves, and his lips lifted in an appreciative smile. "But you're probably just as good."

She shook her head in mock disapproval. "Is that all you can think about?"

"Well, right now I'm hungry. But then . . ."

As she got ready for bed two days later, Laura couldn't say *exactly* what made her uncomfortable around Brandon's mother. Carol McGuire was a widow in her early sixties who looked almost a decade younger. It was obvious from her trim figure, beautifully manicured nails and carefully colored soft blond hair that she took excellent care of herself. Her knit suits and sensible but stylish shoes were in the best of taste. And she treated Laura with what was almost warmth. But that was precisely the problem. There was something under the surface of her polished manners—something that the younger woman couldn't quite put her finger on.

Laura pulled her nightgown over her head and stood staring at her reflection in the old-fashioned cheval mirror that had occupied a corner of her bedroom since she was a little girl.

Trying to be objective, she studied her features. She might never have dared to call herself beautiful before. But now she could see delicate beauty in her own face. It had a lot to do with her love for Brandon, she knew. It shone in her eyes, giving her a glow, a vitality, that had been missing for so many years.

What did Carol McGuire see when she looked at that same face? Laura wondered. Brandon's mother hadn't met Laura Carson before, didn't know the person she had been, and doubtless didn't understand how her son had changed her life. Or maybe she had decided that was no real concern of hers.

From Mrs. McGuire's guarded manner, Laura suspected that the older woman saw her son's fiancée as some sort of threat. But then, maybe that was natural. What mother gladly gave up her son—particularly her only son—to another woman, even if it was the second time around?

Gnawing thoughtfully on her lower lip, Laura ran through her encounters with the older woman.

They had met for the first time at Baltimore-Washington International Airport. Waiting nervously at Brandon's side, Laura had scanned the faces of the passengers coming up the exit ramp. It wasn't hard to spot Carol McGuire. She was looking for her son. As soon as she located him in the crowd, her eyes flicked for a moment to the woman whose fingers were meshed with his. But her look of warm, motherly pleasure was reserved for Brandon, and she kept her gaze focused on him as she hurried purposefully forward.

"It's good to see you so soon again," she murmured, stepping back to survey his smiling face and then his navy blazer and gray slacks with obvious maternal approval.

"Mom, I'd like you to meet Laura," he prompted, turning to put his arm around his fiancée's shoulder.

"Oh, yes. Laura. It's so good to finally meet you after hearing so much about you," Mrs. McGuire said. "Brandon called to let me know about your engagement. Congratulations."

The words sounded friendly, but the inspection the older woman gave her future daughter-in-law was mostly curious.

"Brandon just can't stop talking about you," she added, stepping forward to give Laura a quick little hug that ended almost before it began.

"And I've heard a lot about you, too," Laura returned, fighting the awkward feeling that made her want to cling tightly to Brandon's elbow. She hadn't had much experience with this kind of encounter. Perhaps meeting one's future mother-in-law was always awkward.

Most of the talk on the way back was of mutual friends and acquaintances in Chicago. And every time Brandon tried to enlarge the scope of the conversation to include Laura, somehow the chatter always seemed to return to its original, narrow channel.

"I'm afraid I didn't make much of an impression," Laura whispered as Brandon dropped her off at home before taking his mother back to his house to settle in.

He laughed. "That's just Mother's way. She thinks that Chicago is the center of the universe. But don't worry. There will be plenty of time for the two of you to get to know each other."

Laura told herself he was right. But she couldn't help sensing an ever so slight edge of disapproval in many of the older woman's comments. That evening, when mother and son came to Laura's home for dinner, Mrs. McGuire looked with interest at the eclectic collection of furnishings that Laura had always thought of as charming.

"My, what a mix of styles," she mused. "I see somewhat the same trend at Brandon's. Is that your influence?"

"Why, I don't know."

"Don't blame it on Laura, Mother. You know I've always had pretty strong ideas about making the environment I live in comfortable."

"Yes, I do remember when you were a boy you used to rearrange the furniture in your room every couple of months. I never knew when I walked in whether your bureau would be over by the window or if you'd be using your desk for a bedside table."

Laura turned to Brandon. "Did you really do that?"

"Oh, yes," his mother answered. "And that's just one of the things he probably hasn't told you." For the next ten minutes she went on to describe some of the inevitable childhood scrapes he'd gotten into.

Laura found the recitation amusing. "So why *did* you put salt in the sugar bowl in the teacher's dining room?" she asked.

Brandon looked at his mother for a moment. "I thought I'd explained that to you at the time. The faculty had voted to cancel the Easter vacation trip to Washington, D.C. Salting the sugar seemed like a perfectly reasonable retaliation to a fourteen-year-old kid."

"Well, the principal didn't think so," Mrs. McGuire murmured.

Was Brandon's mother consciously trying to give her second thoughts? Laura wondered later. Or was the older woman simply reacting to what she saw as a rivalry between herself and her daughter-in-law-to-be? In a way that made sense. Maybe she instinctively felt that a younger, more vital woman was taking over from her, and she was reflexively holding on to what she had.

The older woman's losing battle was a bit sad, Laura realized. She and Brandon were already committed to each other. And nothing could tear them apart. If she couldn't win his mother over before the wedding, it would just have to be a gradual process afterward.

Meanwhile, unfortunately, Laura had her own frustrations to deal with. Sighing, she turned down her sheets, looking regretfully at her empty double bed. Brandon had spent the night here with her before. But that was out of the question with his mother staying at his house. It was equally out of the question that she share his bed now—or come over for one of their very intimate trysts in the hot tub that Carson's had installed in a corner of the deck.

The first evening the tub had been in operation, Laura had come over to find a miniature sailing ship—complete with twin masts and billowing rigging—floating in the heated water.

Turning to Brandon, she grinned. "So that's how you plan to use your expensive new appliance—as a pond for your toy boat. I might have known it would bring out the little boy in you."

He watched as she perched on the side of the tub and rippled her hand through the water, making the toy craft bob and sway. "Actually, it accomplished its purpose. It was really a lure to get you over to the water."

Before she had time to think about his provocative words, he crossed the deck and sat down beside her on the wooden ledge. In the next moment, he reached out and began to unbutton her blouse.

"But it's not even dark," she protested, looking around in consternation. Brandon's deck was completely private. And the hot tub itself was screened by a low latticework railing as well as the surrounding woods. Yet Laura's upbringing was very conventional, and she would never have thought of undressing outdoors and simply climbing in.

Brandon grinned. "But we're quite alone here. Unless you count that guy across the valley with the binoculars." He pointed to a distant outcropping of rock on the far rim of the canyon.

Quickly Laura raised her eyes and followed the direction Brandon indicated before turning back to him. "You're teasing me," she accused.

"Yup."

He had already finished with the buttons on her blouse. And soon she forgot about everything but the fiery sensations he was evoking with his lips and hands. By the time he had helped her out of the rest of her clothing and shed his own jeans and shirt, she was ready for anything he had in mind. And once they were in the azure water, it wasn't long until she found out just how inventive his imagination could be.

"I suppose you had all this planned when you asked me to put this hot tub in," she mused much later, watching as he gave the bobbing boat a lazy shove with his toes.

"How did you guess?"

"I'm beginning to understand how your mind works, Mr. McGuire."

"Good."

He gave her a quick kiss. "Actually, I bought the boat for another reason. I was wondering if you'd like to try a sailing trip some time."

Laura looked up at him quizzically. "I've never been sailing. How do you know I'd be any good at it?"

He seemed to give the question serious consideration as he sent the little boat bobbing once more. "You're so good at learning new things," he finally murmured. "I have every confidence in you."

She splashed him playfully then.

And naturally he retaliated.

"Besides, we can get a lot of practice here first," he murmured when he had finally captured her in his arms again. And it was a long time before they remembered they hadn't yet eaten dinner.

That was the kind of warm, close evening Laura missed so desperately now. But they had talked about it and agreed that there was no way she could flaunt their physical relationship in front of Mrs. McGuire. Yet she wished the man she loved were there to pull her close and reassure her that she could indeed turn his mother into an ally.

After fluffing up her pillows, Laura leaned back and stared up at the old familiar crack in the ceiling that had always reminded her of the Big Dipper. Maybe she was reacting more strongly to this motherly inspection tour than she should.

Laura closed her eyes and snuggled down under the covers. Maybe all it would take to win over Mrs. McGuire was a resolutely friendly manner and some careful reassurances that she didn't intend to usurp her future mother-in-law's place in her son's life.

The next day, when Brandon stopped by the garden center just before noon, she was given an opportunity to start putting her plan into practice.

"Mom's busy shopping. But she asked me to tell you she wants to have lunch with you Thursday—just the two of you. She's made reservations at the Harmond House."

"That sounds wonderful," Laura agreed. "I'll call her

this evening and tell her I'm looking forward to it. Actually, I was wondering when the two of us were going to have some time together."

"She seems to like you," Brandon reassured her.

"I hope so."

"Well, I like you," he added. "And I haven't seen much of you lately, so I thought we might pick up some sandwiches at Tony's and go back to my house for lunch."

Laura glanced at her watch. "We're pretty busy today. But I think I can take an hour off to spend with you."

Brandon looked a bit disappointed. "Well, if that's all the time you can spare."

"I'm sorry. But a shipment of summer bedding stock came in a few minutes ago, and we have to get it sorted before customers start coming in looking for the dwarf marigolds and the pink petunias. If everything's all in a jumble, people are likely to go somewhere else for their flowers. And I couldn't blame them."

"All right, I'll settle for what I can get," Brandon grumbled.

"I suspect lunch wasn't the only thing you had in mind," Laura pointed out as she climbed up into the Blazer and pulled the door shut.

Brandon turned her toward him. "What I really want is to take you to bed and devour you—or warm you up in the hot tub. But if I have to settle for a sandwich and a little kissing and hugging, I guess I'll manage."

Laura reached out to stroke his cheek. "I wish I could stay for something more, too. I missed you last night."

"Me too." He reached over to run his fingers through her hair. "Are you sure you can't spare me the afternoon?"

"Sorry," she repeated, her expression wistful.

"Okay. I'll stop trying to make you feel guilty. Anyway, Mom will be going home Friday, and I intend to hold you captive in my bed all weekend."

Laura moved over to rest her head on his shoulder for a moment as they pulled into Tony's tree-shaded parking lot.

"Brandon, would you be angry if we just ate here?" she asked.

He turned toward her and raised a questioning eyebrow.

"If we go to your house, I'm going to be tempted to make this a naked lunch. And I really can't let Sylvia down."

"Yeah," he breathed huskily. "I'd probably just start putting more pressure on you the minute we stepped inside the door. You're right. We should eat here."

Nevertheless, when they returned to the car after their meal, Brandon hesitated for a moment before starting the engine.

"What are you doing?" Laura questioned.

"This." Hauling her across the foot of space that separated them, he found her lips with his, tasting her with a hunger that could not be appeased until they were really alone. As always, she reacted to him just as strongly. When his hands massaged her arms and then traveled to the front of her blouse to cup her breasts for just a moment, she couldn't repress a little moan of pleasure.

"This is driving me crazy," he groaned when he finally tore his mouth away from hers.

"Yes."

He pulled her back into his arms and again they were lost in the taste and touch of each other. This time, it was harder for them to wrench their lips apart.

Laura found it difficult to keep from trembling. Brandon simply leaned his head against the back of the seat and closed his eyes. As he shifted his knee, it collided with the volume control on the radio. Suddenly, a rock and roll song that had been playing quietly in the background blared out at them.

"Hey, babe, let's do it . . ." an impassioned tenor wailed.

Brandon's burst of laughter was followed quickly by Laura's.

"Well, that guy's certainly got the right idea," he chuckled.

Laura nodded, flushing slightly as she realized where they were. What if someone had come out of Tony's and seen them? she wondered.

"Well, since we're not going to take the song's advice, I'd better get you back," Brandon sighed. "But don't expect me to get out of the car and come in for a chat with Sylvia—congenial though she is."

"I won't. This is just as hard for me as it is for you, you know."

He laughed. "I doubt it."

"Figuratively, I mean."

As they pulled into Carson's parking lot, Laura turned to him. "Oh, I forgot. Thursday night I'm going to that meeting with Kramer's people."

"Since you hadn't mentioned it lately, I was beginning to hope he'd given up and canceled it."

"Wishful thinking. But I do suspect he's had trouble getting as much support as he'd like for his viewpoint. However, now that he's finally making some sort of presentation, I intend to give the other side."

"Needless to say, I wish you good luck. You know I'd like to go too," he added.

"But you can't. This has to be all local people talking the issues out among themselves."

Brandon nodded. "I understand. But I'll expect a full report when you get back."

"Naturally."

Thursday morning, Laura took extra time deciding how to dress. Finally she settled on a soft mint green shirtwaist and matching sling-back pumps. The outfit looked dressy enough for lunch at the Harmond House.

But she'd still be able to wear it back to the garden center that afternoon—if she stayed away from the dirty work. And if she didn't have time to change, it would even be suitable for her evening meeting.

What exactly did Brandon's mother want to talk about? she wondered as she brushed on soft gray eye shadow and drew a fine charcoal line just above her lashes.

Over the week, the two women had gotten to know each other a bit better. Mrs. McGuire seemed more relaxed, more accepting. She'd even agreed to help Laura and Brandon pick out some casual furniture for his recreation room. But Laura still detected some subtle lack of enthusiasm in the older woman's manner that made her afraid to let down her own guard completely.

Well, maybe at lunch she'd finally find out what was on Carol McGuire's mind, Laura decided as she stood back to survey her handiwork. The makeup was subtle, yet it brought out the best in her features. She felt a little as though she'd just put on battle armor for her meeting with Brandon's mother. The attractive face staring back at her in the mirror did make her feel a bit more self-assured.

When Laura walked into the Harmond House, her future mother-in-law was already seated in the small vestibule.

"I hope I didn't keep you waiting," Laura murmured, as the older woman got to her feet.

"Not at all. I was worried about finding the place, so I left a little early."

"Do you have a quiet table where we could talk?" she asked the hostess as they were led into the dining room.

"How about this booth in the back?"

"Perfect."

"Well, would you like a cocktail before we order?" Mrs. McGuire asked as they looked over the menu.

Laura shook her head. "No. I have to get back to the

garden center this afternoon. And a cocktail would probably make me sleepy."

For a few moments, they each mulled over the restaurant's selections in silence. When Mrs. McGuire chose a salad plate, Laura decided to have the same thing.

"Oh, don't feel you have to have a salad just because I'm ordering one," the older woman insisted.

"No, I'm really not all that hungry," Laura explained. In fact, she was feeling too tense to eat much.

During the first part of the meal, Mrs. McGuire kept the conversation light and inconsequential. As they talked about Harperstown and gardening, Laura began to wonder why the other woman had requested this luncheon meeting.

Finally, Mrs. McGuire cleared her throat. "You know, my dear, over the past week I've been able to see how devoted you are to Brandon."

"Yes."

"You love him very much, don't you?"

Laura nodded. This praise of her devotion was certainly not what she had expected.

"Well, that's something we have in common," his mother went on. "I also love my son very much. And I want to know that he's really going to be happy."

"I think we are going to be happy," Laura assured her. "We have so much in common. We respect each other's abilities and opinions. We hardly ever fight. And I think we really do have a lot to give each other."

Mrs. McGuire's eyes sought the younger woman's. "I realize all that. But there's more to marriage than just two people living together." She paused for a moment. "Has he spoken to you about his first marriage—and about what happened?"

Laura was shocked. How could Brandon's mother ask such a question? "Of course. We don't have any secrets from each other."

"Oh, I'm sure he told you the facts," Mrs. McGuire

went on. "But I don't think you realize what his wife and his son meant to him. You didn't see the look of pride on his face when he brought them home from the hospital. Or watch him help bathe that little baby, or feed him or walk the floor with him at night. And you didn't live through the months of anguish with him after the accident when he lost both his son and his wife."

Laura had gone pale, suddenly remembering the album she had found the day she had helped Brandon unpack. She had been well aware of the look on his face in those pictures—and the pain in his eyes when he had touched the image of his dead son.

"Having a child was obviously very important to Brandon," his mother went on. "And it's still important, even if he doesn't realize it or won't admit it now."

"But we did talk about it. He told me—" Laura began, afraid of what this woman might say, and even more afraid of what she had seen in Brandon's eyes that day.

"I'm sure he tried to convince you that it doesn't matter. And maybe he's even convinced himself—for the time being. But I'm his mother. I know him. I know what he wants and what he needs." There was real anguish in the older woman's voice as she continued. "Laura, you're a charming woman, a lovely person. I know why Brandon was attracted to you. And if circumstances were different . . ." She let the sentence trail off meaningfully.

Laura had known something was bothering Carol McGuire. But she was completely unprepared for this. Brandon's mother was playing on the old doubts and fears Laura had struggled so hard to conquer.

"There is something important you can't give him," Mrs. McGuire continued now. "And I can't help believing that if he marries you, he'll regret what he gave up five or six or ten years down the line. How would you feel then?"

Laura didn't know how she might feel in five or ten years. She only knew that right now she felt as though someone had just hit her in the chest with a wrecking ball.

Suddenly it was hard to breathe. What was Mrs. McGuire asking of her? But she knew.

Raising anxious blue eyes, she forced herself to search the older woman's face, finding pain there, but also determination.

Despite everything, some part of Laura was still fighting back. "You can't stop me from marrying Brandon," she insisted, struggling to keep her voice from giving away the fear that had suddenly gripped her body.

"No, I can't," Mrs. McGuire acknowledged. "But if you love my son as much as you say, you'll do what's best for him."

Unfortunately, it was an argument Laura simply didn't know how to counter. She did love Brandon—with all her heart and soul. She did want to do what was best for him. But at what cost to herself?

Mrs. McGuire could see the inner struggle reflected in Laura's face and was quick to press the advantage it gave her.

"You've given Brandon something very special, and I'll always be grateful to you for bringing him out of his grief," she murmured, as though the issue had already been decided. "But he has to go on from here. He needs a wife who can give him the family that means so much to him. You can't deny him that, can you?"

It was hard for Laura to focus through the film of tears blurring her vision. They threatened to spill out onto her cheeks. And that was the last thing she wanted to have happen in front of Carol McGuire.

"Excuse me," she mumbled, scraping back her chair. And then she was dashing headlong through the restaurant, almost tumbling over several chairs in her haste to get away.

After fumbling with the lock on her car, she climbed inside and collapsed with her head in her hands against the steering wheel, unable now to hold back the flood of anguished tears streaming down her cheeks.

Her first impulse was to go to Brandon. Like a lost

child, she wanted to seek the reassurance of his strong arms.

Yet instead of giving comfort, the image only brought forth a fresh torrent of misery. What good would it do to run to Brandon now? He might soothe her for the moment, but what would it all really mean? Mrs. McGuire had brought into sharp focus what she'd been afraid of all along. Laura knew Brandon wanted her now. She was certain of that. But what about later when he realized what he had given up? He might very well grow to hate her for having cheated him of something very precious— something he could still have with another woman but not with her.

10

Laura had intended to spend the afternoon at the garden center, but there was no way she could face Sylvia—or anyone else—at the moment.

Instead, with tears still streaming down her face, she somehow managed to drive home. By the time she had pulled into the parking place next to the back door, she had made a decision. Still, it took her many minutes to get enough control of her emotions to call Sylvia.

But she couldn't fool her old friend. "What's wrong?" the garden center's manager asked her immediately. It sounded as though Laura was hanging on to her control by only a slender thread.

"Sylvia, I just don't think I can talk about it right now."

"What can I do to help?" the older woman offered, her heart contracting in response to the anguish she could now sense on the other end of the line. Laura answered only the immediate question.

"I don't quite know how to ask this, but do you think

you can manage Carson's alone for a while? I-I have to get away, and I'm not sure for how long."

Sylvia was as unprepared for the request as she had been for Laura's obvious distress. That morning, when the two of them had conferred over the phone, Laura had been a bit nervous at the prospect of meeting alone with her future mother-in-law, but her spirits had been basically high. And then it struck her. "What happened at lunch with Mrs. McGuire?" she asked quietly.

"I . . . she . . ." Laura began, but she couldn't finish. "Let me call you back later," she gasped, hanging up the phone and sinking down onto the couch, her shoulders shaking as uncontrollable sobs racked her slender body once again. That was how Sylvia found her fifteen minutes later.

Sylvia tiptoed into the living room, sat down beside Laura and pulled the distraught young woman into her arms. "It's all right. It's going to be all right," she soothed, rocking her back and forth as though she were a distressed child.

But Laura could only shake her head. It wasn't going to be all right, not now, not ever.

When finally there were no more tears to be shed, Sylvia handed Laura a tissue.

"I know you'd probably like me to leave you alone," she said, "but I'm not going to until I find out what's happened."

Laura looked at the determination in her friend's eyes. Clearly, the older woman wasn't going to leave until she found out what had caused all the misery. It was still hard for Laura to speak of something so painful, but in little bits and pieces, Sylvia pried out an account of what had happened at lunch.

"Why, that meddling old witch," she gasped when she had finally heard the whole story. "I can't believe she would say something so cruel to you."

"But it's true, you know."

"Bull!"

Laura shook her head. "Sylvia, we both know I can't give Brandon children. I've been telling myself it didn't matter. But now I finally realize how selfish it would be to tie him down. In time he'll get over me. Then he'll be able to find someone who can really fulfill his needs."

Sylvia looked at Laura's bowed head and slumping shoulders. Was she really going to give up the man she loved on this sort of evidence? "Brandon's a grown man, you know," she argued. "Are you trying to tell me that his mother knows better than he does what he needs?"

Laura shook her head sadly. "It's not just what his mother says. Brandon met me at a time when he was very vulnerable. He thinks he knows what he wants now, but she's right. If he married me, five or ten years down the line he'd probably—"

"Why don't you stop speculating and talk to the man about this?" Sylvia broke in. "After all, I'd say he's rather intimately involved."

"I think it's better not to talk to him. I already know what he'd say." And then another thought struck her. "And don't you talk to him about it either. You've got to promise me that."

Sylvia nodded slowly. If Laura wanted to extract such a promise, so be it. She'd comply for the sake of peace now. But she'd have to give some serious thought to whether she was really going to be bound by such self-destructive nonsense.

"I've got to get away from Brandon's influence—away from here," Laura said. "My parents have been asking me to visit them in New Mexico again. I think I'll call and see if they'd mind my coming out there on short notice— I mean as soon as I can throw some clothes in a suitcase."

Sylvia raised an eyebrow. "Aren't you forgetting something important?" she asked.

"What?"

"Isn't Kramer's big meeting tonight?"

Laura slapped her hand to her forehead. "My God,

Sylvia, you're right. I'd forgotten all about it. I have to go. I told Brandon I would, and it's the least I can do for him under the circumstances."

Privately, Sylvia was thinking that there was certainly a lot more Laura could do for Brandon. But she could see that arguing the matter further would get her nowhere right now. Laura's wounds were too fresh for her to put things in their proper perspective.

"Is your presentation ready?" she asked.

"Yes. I just have to go over my notes a few more times so I sound as though I know what I'm talking about." Laura's voice had suddenly taken on a much stronger note, as though she were grasping at this chance to push her own bitter disappointment to the back of her mind.

"I guess I'd better get back to the garden center, then," Sylvia murmured.

Laura looked up at the other woman. "I appreciate your coming over."

Her friend nodded.

"But there's something else you have to do for me," Laura insisted. "In case Brandon calls, I'm not going to answer the phone. And if he happens to phone over there, would you tell him not to call back until tomorrow morning?"

Sylvia looked doubtful. "If that's what you want," she finally agreed.

"Yes. It's what I want."

Laura spent the rest of the afternoon in a flurry of activity—calling her mother, making plane reservations, piling clothes into a suitcase, going over her notes, and planning a tentative strategy for the evening meeting. And during it all, she allowed herself to feel nothing. It was as though, in the space of a few hours, the old, self-protective Laura had taken control again. Things weren't going to work out with Brandon after all. But she wasn't going to let that destroy her. She had been strong enough to survive loss once. She would be able to do it again.

By eight o'clock, when she pulled into the parking lot at the West Side Community Center where Hal Kramer was holding his meeting, she was feeling as calm as the surface of a pond on a windless day.

She had changed from the green dress she'd worn at lunch into a conservative blue suit and gray blouse. She had told herself that it better suited the image she wanted to project when she gave her presentation. But in reality, she felt more comfortable without that reminder of the painful interview with Mrs. McGuire.

Although Laura was only a few minutes late, the large room was just under half-full when she entered. Hal Kramer had apparently expected a bigger turnout. Maybe he didn't have as much support for his position as he'd led Tim to believe, Laura mused.

If the business leader was disappointed in the turnout, however, he didn't let it dampen his enthusiasm. He was standing near the door, greeting each new arrival by name and exchanging pleasantries in a booming voice. His eyes lit up when he spotted Laura waiting her turn to approach the one-man reception line.

"Glad you decided to join us," he approved robustly, patting her on the back and ushering her forward. "I'm sure you know everybody here."

Laura forced herself not to shrink from the unwelcome personal contact. Pretending a great interest in the crowd, she looked around. Kramer was right. Most of the attendees were men and women she recognized from the downtown business community, with a smattering of suburban merchants like herself. Tim nodded to her and she acknowledged the greeting.

"Brought some notes, I see," Kramer commented, looking with ill-disguised curiosity at the folder she had tucked under her arm.

"Yes," she admitted, keeping her voice neutral so as not to give him any clues about her intentions.

Kramer could see that she wasn't going to reveal her position before the meeting. "Well, have some coffee and

159

a pastry," he suggested, affably pointing toward a table that had been set up at the side of the room.

The food made Laura realize that she'd completely forgotten about dinner. But the sight of several men and women sipping coffee from Styrofoam cups and munching on cherry and pineapple danish made her stomach knot painfully. She'd been congratulating herself on how she'd brought her roiling emotions under control. Apparently her body hadn't gotten the message.

"No thanks," she demurred, then moved toward the front of the room and selected a seat several rows from the speaker's podium. She wanted to be visible when she spoke, but she also wanted to be able to see the reactions of at least some of the audience to Hal Kramer's erroneous picture of Brandon's plans.

The community leader waited several more minutes before coming forward to open the meeting. As Laura suspected, he got right to the point.

"I'm delighted to see so many of you here tonight," he began. "I know you all share my concern about what's been happening in downtown Harperstown. And I'm glad you've decided to join me in opposing the inappropriate use of some choice property—and by an outside firm that obviously doesn't understand the needs and problems of our historic community."

Kramer's opening remarks assumed that most of those in the room had already made up their minds against the project. But Laura wondered if that was really the case, or if the man was using the assertion as a persuasive tactic.

She listened carefully as he went on to outline his position, using not only the material from the General Development preliminary report but some half-truths of his own. The whole presentation was designed to leave the impression that Brandon's conference center would be bad for downtown Harperstown and bad for most of the merchants assembled. And worse, Kramer charged that General Development knew perfectly well what it was doing.

When he had finished, there was a smattering of applause from around the room. The speaker smiled his thanks and then looked out over the audience solicitously. "Any questions?" he asked.

Martha Thomas, a well-groomed matron who owned a dress shop in the middle of the downtown shopping district, raised her hand.

"We've been saying for years that we need new development to bring customers back to the central city. Why don't you think this project qualifies?" she asked.

"Because it would create as many problems as it would solve," Kramer asserted, going on to restate his arguments about lack of parking and increased crime.

When he had finished, Carl Richards, a bookstore owner, stood up. "You say General Development is planning to tear down historic buildings. Well, I've seen the block you're referring to. Those townhouses are in bad condition. Some of them are literally falling down already. Finishing the job might be better than allowing them to continue in their present state of disrepair."

His argument brought murmurs of agreement from around the room.

"I know that many of us would like to see those properties restored rather than demolished," Kramer asserted. "That way they'd be a real asset to the downtown area—more so than a modern building, which would be completely out of character for the community."

That observation gave Laura the opportunity she'd been waiting for. Willing the knots in her stomach to relax, she raised her hand.

Kramer turned to her with his best smile. "Do you have something to add to that assessment?"

"Yes, I do," Laura said, standing up and forcing herself to look around the room calmly. "After Tim Warfield approached me last month about this whole issue, I became interested enough to ask some questions. One thing I found out is that Tim had gotten his information from General Development's own corporate offices. But he only had a copy of their preliminary report, which went into great detail on the problems the company might encounter in trying to develop its conference center here."

There was a murmur of agreement in the audience. Apparently Kramer had made sure the report was well circulated.

Laura waited for the noise to subside before going on. "However, that was only General Development's initial and very candid assessment of the pitfalls they'd encounter. Since then they've come up with solutions to most of the problems—solutions which are spelled out in a later report."

The statement brought forth a buzz of conversation, and Laura had to wait some time before the room was once more quiet. "For example, although the townhouses in question were originally thought unsalvageable, most are now slated for renovation and restoration. General Development is prepared to go to considerable expense to save them. The only buildings that would be torn down are those that are simply beyond saving."

The crowd gave her its complete attention now. Laura found that most of her nervousness had disappeared. She had gone over this material until she was sure she could deliver a smooth presentation. Without even referring to her notes, she went on to outline General Development's plans, describing their solutions to the sewage, parking and traffic problems, the new building slated for construction, and the outdoor courtyard that would benefit local residents as well as those attending the conference center.

"So you see," she concluded, "the facility would help revitalize the center of Harperstown without detracting from the historic character of the area. It would be good for business and therefore benefit most of you."

There was another flurry of questions when Laura

finished. Most simply required clarification of the points she'd already made. From the excited and friendly tenor of the response, it was obvious that her presentation had been persuasive.

But Hal Kramer wasn't about to let her turn the tide so easily.

"And just how did you get such, uh . . . intimate access to General Development's plans?" he asked, a slightly suggestive note in his voice. Laura knew it was meant to be a warning.

"I don't have any privileged information," she forced herself to return smoothly. "The company isn't making a secret of its intentions. In fact, General Development has filed an updated report with the county zoning board. Anybody who wants to see it can have free access."

She would have liked to have sat down, but Kramer didn't give her the chance. He was out to discredit her presentation. And if one method didn't work, he'd try another.

"If General Development is being so open and above-board, why did they use covert methods to acquire the property they wanted? Why didn't they simply announce their intentions from the outset?" he pressed.

"Isn't it obvious? It was simply good business sense. They knew property values would shoot up if they advertised what they were doing beforehand."

Laura saw several members of the audience nod their agreement. Kramer saw it too and decided to mount an attack in earnest. "I have reason to think that your interest in all this is more . . . personal than you've led us to believe. Haven't you been seeing a lot of General Development's chief honcho in the area? I believe his name is Brandon McGuire—although he hasn't made himself personally known to me."

The words made Laura's heart lurch. The last thing she wanted was to discuss her private relationship with Brandon in public. Her knuckles whitening on the chair in front of her, she fought hard to keep a grip on her self-control. Bowing her head for a moment, she forced herself to breathe deeply and evenly.

Around her, she could hear the buzz of curious conversation that had started up in the auditorium. It would be easy, she realized, to interpret her reaction as guilt. If she were there only for herself, she might have turned and fled. But she couldn't let Brandon down. With her lips set in a determined line, she raised her face to Kramer.

"Are you trying to suggest," she asked quietly, "that I would come here and present a point of view I didn't believe in?"

Her opponent shrugged with elaborate casualness, yet Laura could see the tension in his shoulders. "I'm not trying to suggest anything. But you've got to admit that it looks as if you have ulterior motives."

Laura could sense a murmur of agreement rippling through the room.

She was really no match for a man like Hal Kramer, she realized. He'd been using underhanded debating tactics for years, and this was her first foray into the public arena. Her only hope would be to end the discussion quickly with a decisive blow. Taking another deep breath and letting it out slowly, she forced herself to look calm even though she knew that she was now skating on thin ice.

"Well then, let me ask you a question," she began innocently. "If you think destroying the historic character of the area is such a bad idea, why did you consult a development firm several months ago about the feasibility of locating a new hotel in the same area?"

That brought an even louder rumble of excitement from the audience.

Kramer was taken by surprise, as she'd hoped he would be. "I haven't consulted any development firms," he blurted defensively. "I'd only started investigating the possibility of locating a hotel in the area when McGuire came in and . . ." He stopped abruptly, realizing what he had said.

Laura released the breath she'd been holding. "Then if you already thought a hotel complex in the center of town was a good idea, your interest in seeing the General Development project fail isn't exactly motivated by what's best for Harperstown, is it?"

Kramer recovered his poise quickly. "I don't believe you can prove that."

He might be right, but his protestation was too late. The damage had already been done. Laura heard a snort of amusement from Sam Fitzgerald, the owner of several restaurants in the area. "Oh, come on, Kramer," he gibed, "you'd send Harperstown up the creek in a leaky canoe if you thought it would help you make a buck."

There were snickers from around the auditorium.

Kramer's eyes blazed. But it was clear that the mood of the crowd had shifted. Now the private conversations in the audience were so loud that it took several minutes before Laura could command the crowd's attention again.

"You all know that I've been urging urban redevelopment in Harperstown for years—even though my own business would gain little direct benefit," she began. "I think the General Development plan is a good one. And it has the advantage of bringing some badly needed capital into the area. If you have any questions about what the company is planning, I'm sure Brandon McGuire will be glad to answer them." After giving his phone number and address, she sat down.

To her surprise, a smattering of applause began around the room and then grew louder.

"Thanks for letting us in on the other side of the picture," Tim Warfield said when he could finally be heard.

Laura nodded self-consciously. She hadn't pictured

the focus of attention shifting to herself quite like this. Now that her presentation was over, all she wanted to do was get away.

She looked up to see Tim hurrying up the aisle toward her. "That was quite an eye-opener," he said. "You asked me how I got on the same side of an issue as Kramer. Now I know—he tricked me."

"Don't feel bad," Laura commiserated. "At first glance, that report looked pretty convincing. But once I started digging below the surface, I realized there was more to it."

Tim nodded. "Got time for a cup of coffee?" he asked. "Some of us would like to talk more about this new project with you."

Laura smiled weakly and shook her head. "No, I'm really exhausted." It was true. She had expended all her energy on the presentation. Suddenly she felt as limp as a jellyfish being swept along in a heavy tide. Now that her public performance was over, it was a tremendous effort just to keep her shoulders from sagging.

Tim nodded sympathetically, misinterpreting the reason for her sudden change of mood. "I know you haven't done much public speaking in the past, but we all appreciate your making the effort this evening."

"Thanks," Laura murmured. "But I really do have to go. I have a hectic day ahead of me."

Tim wasn't ready to give up. "Could we talk about this some more tomorrow perhaps?" he pressed.

"I'm afraid I'm going out of town first thing in the morning—to visit my mother and father in New Mexico. Why don't you call Brandon McGuire? I'm sure he'll be glad to give you any information you want."

Despite her resolve to slip away quietly, it was almost a half hour later before Laura made it out the door. Hal Kramer, on the other hand, had lost no time in gliding out of the auditorium like a shadow.

Many of the people who had attended the meeting wanted to thank Laura for giving the other side of the picture. Several were frankly gleeful that she'd blown the whistle on Kramer's private little scheme. And quite a number wanted more information about Brandon McGuire and General Development.

Through all the praise and commotion, Laura remained standing with a smile plastered across her lips. But it didn't reach her eyes.

It had been necessary to give Brandon's phone number and address to the audience. But now the constant stream of questions about him washed over her like storm-driven waves buffeting an unprotected beach.

Every time his name came up in the conversation, she had to brace herself to keep from bolting from the room. She kept seeing Brandon's ruggedly masculine face, remembering snatches of conversation between them, imagining that she could feel the caress of his voice, or the touch of his hand on her shoulder.

No one else realized what was wrong, but they could see the outward effects. Several times Laura had to ask that questions be repeated because she hadn't heard them the first time.

Finally Sam Fitzgerald took pity on her. "Standing up to Kramer the way this little lady did has obviously taken a lot out of her. I think we'd better let her go home and get some rest," he urged.

Laura turned to him with grateful thanks.

But it was no better when she finally gained the privacy of her car. Suddenly she was alone with no distractions and no focus for the rest of the evening.

As she turned on the ignition, the radio sprang to life. Playing softly was the suggestive song she and Brandon had laughed about after they'd gone to lunch. It had been only a few days ago. But it might have been a century.

Reaching out, she snapped off the music. And then, her lip clamped between her teeth, she backed out of the parking space and headed home.

11

The high boxwood hedge that lined the long driveway seemed to press in against Laura as she maneuvered her car toward the house. At the end of the narrow lane, she climbed out and looked around at the house and yard, seeing the spot where her childhood swing set had stood, the rose garden that had been her mother's pride, the upstairs window where she'd watched eagerly for Arthur Henderson—and then Brandon McGuire.

She had lived there all her life and taken this place for granted. But suddenly the painful memories it held seemed to press in against her just as the boxwoods did.

For a moment she had to fight a rising feeling of irrational panic. All at once it was hard to breathe. Leaning back against the cold metal of the car door, she closed her eyes and willed herself to focus on the simple process of drawing air into her lungs and expelling it again. In a few moments she felt somewhat better, but the dizzy sensation remained in the background of her consciousness. And she knew that the more disturbing feeling of helplessness would return if she stayed there much longer. She knew it was because the situation with Brandon was no longer under her control. And she couldn't cope with that.

Climbing the wooden steps to the side porch, she looked at her watch in the light from the bulb above the door. Her plane reservation was for nine-thirty the next morning. If she could have changed it to a flight that evening, she would have.

Her parents' home in New Mexico had never seemed more like a refuge. She had visited before and felt almost as though she were in a foreign land. The high desert country and rugged mountains were alien to her experience, as were the flat, earth-colored adobe architecture and the landscaping that featured as many rocks as plants. The air was different, and even the sky was an almost unreal, more intense blue. Surely in that setting, which was so different from the familiar locale of Harperstown, she could get a better grip on her equanimity.

But it wasn't just the environment that was causing Laura's distress. As she undressed for bed, she happened to glance down at her left hand. There, staring back at her like a blinking searchlight, was the diamond solitaire that Brandon had given her a week ago.

For a moment she took in the fiery beauty of the perfectly cut gem. Then with trembling fingers, she slipped off the reminder of what she was giving up and clenched it tightly for a moment in her fist. It must be returned to Brandon, of course. She had no right to this symbol of their engagement now. But it wasn't something she could put in the mail. It would just have to stay in her jewelry box for the time being.

Laura couldn't remember getting any sleep that night. She could take off Brandon's ring, but she couldn't stop the images of the past few months from flickering through her mind. It had been a very special time for her—like nothing else she had ever experienced in her life. And now that she was no longer in a crowded meeting hall, the memories were more private and more painful. Some were so warm and tender and loving that she felt her heart constrict in her chest. It was an effort to keep from reaching out and picking up the phone to call Brandon.

Her thoughts would come back to the afternoon he'd first told her about the loss of his wife and baby, or the time when she'd found that album full of pictures of a laughing, vibrantly alive baby named Jason. And always her shell-shocked brain drew the same conclusion. Brandon had told her that he hadn't really come to terms with what he had lost in the past. When that day finally arrived, he would almost certainly realize he wanted a wife who could give him a family. And then her time with him would have run out.

Could she settle for a few years of happiness with him? she asked herself. But she knew the answer to that question. Having Brandon and then losing him would simply be postponing unimaginable pain. It was really better to end things now while she was still young enough to pull her life back together. And yet, that was no comfort as she tried to cope with her present anguish.

Finally, at six, she sat up and turned off her alarm. All this agonizing was getting her nowhere. She might as well get ready now and leave for the airport instead of torturing herself this way.

The bathroom mirror showed her a face she hardly recognized. There were dark smudges under her eyes, and her skin had a drawn, chalky look. But she felt too dispirited to bother camouflaging the outward signs of her inner turmoil. Instead she quickly washed her face and ran a comb through her hair before pulling on a simple blue shirtwaist dress and slipping into a pair of sandals.

The very thought of eating breakfast made her stomach knot. She forced herself to sip a cup of tea before stowing her two suitcases in the trunk of her Toyota.

Without glancing back at the house, she turned the key in the ignition and started down the narrow, rutted drive with more speed than usual, intent on getting away from that place as soon as possible. As she rounded a blind corner halfway down to the road, she was forced to slam on her brakes. Sitting squarely between the boxwood hedges so that it completely blocked the drive was Brandon's blue and white Blazer. Her own vehicle screeched to a halt only a few feet away, but the near collision didn't seem to phase Brandon, who was sitting calmly in the Blazer's driver's seat.

Laura couldn't repress a gasp. Brandon McGuire was the last person she had expected—or wanted to see— that morning.

She eyed him cautiously as he opened the door and got out of the car. His actions seemed casual, but Laura knew him too well. She could detect signs of tension in the way he moved as he came toward her. His shirt was rumpled, she noted, as though he had been wearing it all night. His hair was barely combed. And the dark circles under her own eyes seemed to be reflected by twin smudges under his.

"Get out," he ordered, bending down toward her open window. The roughness in his voice was another clue to his emotional state. "I want to talk to you."

"Well, it should be obvious that I don't want to talk to you," she shot back, trying to convey her defiance. But her mouth was so dry that she could hardly get the words out.

"What you want and what's going to happen are two different things," he noted dispassionately, opening the door and reaching in to turn off the engine. Before she could protest, he stuffed her car keys into the pocket of his jeans. Then, grasping her firmly by the elbow, he began to lead her back toward the house. She tried to dig her heels into the ground, but that only made her stumble along the gravel drive. She was too startled by his arrival to put up much of a fight.

"What do you think you're doing?" she challenged.

But he didn't answer.

She asked the question again when he brought her to a halt at the front door and began to rummage in her purse for the house key. Silently he extracted it and inserted it in the lock.

Before she had time to really consider what was happening, Laura found herself back in her living room being pushed down none too gently onto the couch.

After forcing her to sit down, Brandon strode across the room and turned to face her, his features set in harsh lines.

"I remember that the two of us agreed to talk over any problems we were having. Just what right do you have to walk out on me like this without even discussing the matter?"

She wanted to tell him that circumstances had canceled all their agreements, but she didn't quite have the nerve. "What makes you think I was walking out?" she lied instead, willing her voice not to tremble.

"Unfortunately for you, I got it out of Sylvia yesterday evening."

Laura's eyes widened. "But I made her promise—" she began.

"She's not a very good liar," Brandon cut her off sharply in midsentence.

Desperate to make him leave her alone, Laura stood up and looked rebelliously in Brandon's direction. She couldn't quite meet his level gaze. "All right, I was going away . . . because it's all over between us. I don't love you anymore," she managed.

His gaze flicked over her drawn features, the dark smudges under her eyes, the pallor of her skin. And then his obsidian eyes seemed to pierce through to her soul. "You're not a very good liar, either," he bit out, his voice husky with conflicting emotions. "Now sit down. We're going to have this out whether you like it or not."

She wanted to bolt from the room. Why had he come

here? Why was he doing this to her? But she knew that flight was impossible now. She had lost her chance when his Blazer had blocked the drive.

Sighing, she resumed her seat on the sofa. Brandon remained standing, forcing her to look up to address him. He didn't want them on an equal basis. He wanted to keep her at a disadvantage. For a moment, he regarded her appraisingly. "I'm going to start by laying my cards on the table, which is more than you can be credited with." The words had a deliberately baiting quality.

She looked away. It was obvious that he wasn't going to be dissuaded from whatever it was he wanted to say.

"Don't you have any curiosity about why I look as if I've been up all night?" he asked.

"No."

"Well, it's because I've been on the telephone. I started off with Sylvia. Then I talked to your mother in New Mexico. And then I woke up Dr. Grant, the physician who treated you when you had that infection twelve years ago."

Laura's head snapped around. "Just what right did you have to talk to my doctor—or my mother either?" she demanded hotly, wondering just what private information he had managed to acquire. Her heart had begun to thump inside her chest like a jackhammer.

His gaze flicked to her left hand for a moment, noting the absence of the engagement ring he'd given her. But he made no comment about that. "I explained to both of them that I was your fiancé and that you were concerned about your inability to have children," he returned instead.

Laura gripped the arm of the sofa. "Get out of here and leave me alone," she whispered.

He shook his head. "Sorry. I must be a glutton for punishment. This is the second nasty scene I've been through in the past twelve hours. The first one was with my dear mother, after I found out from Sylvia what she had done to you."

Laura tried to open her mouth to speak, but he simply plowed ahead. "What she did might be understandable, since she thought she had her only son's welfare at heart. But it was also inexcusable. And I've made that clear to her in no uncertain terms." And then his obsidian gaze captured Laura's. "And what makes you think my meddling mother knows more about what I want and need than I do myself? After all, I am a grown man, you know."

It was the same question Sylvia had asked yesterday. And Laura's answer had not changed. She had thought about this all night, and she could come to no other conclusion.

She shook her head sadly. This was the confrontation she had tried so desperately to avoid because she knew it couldn't do any good. Now she felt like an accident victim with internal injuries. And she knew she had to get Brandon out of there before she figuratively bled to death. It didn't matter what he *said* to her now. What mattered was the pain in his *eyes* when he'd looked at those pictures of his son.

"Your mother's right," she whispered, aware that if she tried to speak any louder her voice would crack. It was difficult to see Brandon now through the sheen of tears that glazed her eyes. "You may think you want me today, but sooner or later you'd hate me for depriving you of a family."

Brandon swore richly and imaginatively. "Laura, you're an idiot," he growled. "When I told you that I loved you and that having you was more important than having a family, I meant it. And I still do."

She didn't say anything, and Brandon noted the cold, blank look in her eyes. She was deliberately tuning him out—as though that were the only way she could deal with the pain of what she thought was true.

But he wasn't going to allow her to end things so neatly and easily. "Since you're letting your inability to have a child distort your decision-making process," he continued, "you might be interested to know that there have been some almost miraculous advances in the infertility field in the past few years. There are a lot of women who were told they could never have children who are becoming mothers now."

She looked down, simply letting his words wash over her without really hearing what he was saying. All she wanted him to do was leave her alone.

Seeing what she was doing, he crossed the room and grasped her by the shoulders, raising her sharply to her feet. "Dammit, woman, I'm trying to tell you that you might be able to have a baby after all."

But she couldn't take it in. She had made her decision already. She had endured all the pain she could take. And now, all the persuasive arguments in the world weren't going to make her open herself up to anguish again.

In exasperation, Brandon shook her body. "What's wrong with you?" he growled, but she continued to look down at the floor instead of up at him.

"Laura, you're a coward," he grated. "You're giving up your happiness, my happiness, because of a preconceived idea. Don't you know that nothing in this life is sure? There are no ironclad guarantees. For all I know it might have been a thousand-to-one chance that I ever fathered a child in the first place. Maybe I can't have any more children. But it doesn't matter, Laura," he insisted, his voice harsh with emotion. "Don't you see, none of it matters. I love you. I need you. That's what's important. And if you can't see it, you're blind."

Her head was spinning with the effort to shut him out. "If you want to do something for me, just leave me alone," she whispered.

He let go of her shoulders and took a step backwards. Maybe it was the sleepless night he'd spent or the emotional turmoil he'd put himself through, first with his mother and then with Laura. Maybe it was the exasperation of beating his head against a stone wall. Or maybe it was simply that she still didn't trust him, that she was still rejecting his love. But for whatever reason, he suddenly knew he'd reached the end of his will to argue with this woman.

He'd thought he knew her. He'd been elated last night when Dr. Grant had talked to him about all the new advances in the fertility field. Since Laura was so fixated on her barrenness, he'd assumed she'd grasp at that ray of hope. But he had been wrong. She had obviously made up her mind that it was all over between them. And she wasn't going to change it.

This was the woman with whom he'd thought he wanted to spend the rest of his life. But prolonging the bitterness of not being able to reach her was suddenly too much to bear. He turned, walked quickly across the living room and opened the door. Without looking back, he closed it firmly and went down the steps.

For a moment, Laura stood rooted to the spot. She had been prepared for another verbal barrage from Brandon, not for his sudden departure.

She had made him give up. He was leaving. It was finally all over. On leaden legs she crossed the room to look out the window. Brandon stood in the drive, his back still to her. And then he began to walk slowly back to his car.

Now that he had left her, all the fight seemed to have deserted him. Suddenly it was as though she were looking at a different man. She saw the weary sag of his shoulders, the way he walked with his head bent, his muscular arms dangling lifelessly at his sides.

The sight made her chest tighten painfully. And then, in one blinding flash, she realized something so basic and fundamental that her heart seemed to stop. Brandon's posture told her more than all the persuasive words that had just poured out of him.

He was a very physical person. He had made that clear on many occasions. There had been that first night when he'd pulled her into his arms and kissed her because he hadn't been able to communicate in any other way. And the night he had stopped her painful memories by making love to her. And all the other times he had told her with his body what he felt for her.

She had been so convinced that it was wrong to hold on to him, that she hadn't dared to let herself believe in the strength of his commitment to her. But how could she deny the beaten, defeated carriage of his body? This man looked like a refugee from a war-torn country who had lost everything he cared about, everything that was of value to him in life.

How could she doubt that she was important to him—more important than she had ever dared let herself realize?

The weight of her own stubborn stupidity came crashing down around her. And then, with a sudden sick feeling, she remembered what he had told her about rejection the morning after they'd first made love. She had hurt him before by turning him away the night of the auction. But this was far worse. Then he had been trying to forge a bond between them. Now he was seeing their pledge of love shattered.

Bowing her head, she covered her face with her hands. Now at last she realized what she'd done to him in her own desperate struggle to keep from being hurt anymore. She had done everything a woman could to drive her man away. And she knew Brandon might not be able to open himself up to her again. But she also knew that she couldn't simply let him leave now. She had to go after him—if it wasn't already too late, if she hadn't killed his love with her stubborn refusal to trust what he had told her.

She was across the room and out the door almost before she realized she had made her decision.

"Brandon," she called as he was about to disappear around the bend in the drive. "Please, Brandon, don't leave."

He stopped uncertainly and then turned. The look in

his red-rimmed eyes was wary—and angry now. He was silently commanding her to keep her distance, just as she had done with him before. Laura obeyed, coming to an abrupt halt several yards from where he stood.

She felt as though a wad of cotton had settled painfully in her chest, making it hard to speak. She had ignored his words of love and commitment. Her only hope was that he wouldn't do the same thing to her. "Brandon," she began, in a voice that was surprisingly clear and steady, "you were right. I've been a fool. I love you. Please don't leave me, Brandon."

Still he said nothing; after the scene in her living room, he seemed to be the one who couldn't take in what he was hearing.

"I love you," she repeated, putting everything she felt, everything she longed for, into the tone of her voice. More than anything she wanted to close the distance between them and pull him into her arms. But he must make the first move now.

For a heart-stopping moment he seemed to hesitate, searching her face as though he still couldn't believe he had heard her correctly. Then his body was in motion, covering the gap between them in a few decisive steps so that he could pull her into his arms.

"God, Laura, I was sure you'd locked the door on me and thrown the key away," he choked out. At first he pressed her to his hard frame so tightly that she gasped. And then his hands began to roam over her back and up into her hair as if to assure himself that she wouldn't evaporate like the dew that still covered the ground around them. "There's only so much begging a man can do," he added huskily.

The words cut through her. "Oh, Brandon," she groaned. "I thought I had locked you out too. But when I saw the way you looked walking down the driveway, I suddenly knew what a stupid, thick-headed idiot I was being."

"Thank God."

Neither spoke for several seconds. Brandon simply enfolded her in his strength and warmth.

But it was impossible now that she knew he was hers again for Laura to get enough of the comfort and reassurance he offered. "Please just hold me now," she murmured. "I want to know that it's all right again."

"It's all right," he assured her, his hands tangling in her thick dark locks, his lips skimming the top of her head, then brushing against the line of her eyebrows.

She felt a subtle shift in his stance. "Do you just want me to hold you?" he questioned huskily. "Or can I make love to you?" She heard the deep emotion in the question, yet there was an undercurrent of teasing, too. All at once she knew for certain that everything was going to be all right between the two of them.

"Anytime you give me a choice like that, I'm going to pick making love," she promised, tilting her head upward so that he could read the truth of her words in the blue depths of her eyes. The last part of her declaration was spoken with her lips only millimeters from his, so that the warm moistness of their breaths mingled together in the chilly morning air.

They both pressed forward eagerly to complete the physical contact. And as Brandon's lips met hers, it was as though an electrical circuit had been completed. She could feel overwhelming needs and desires flowing from his body to hers and back to him again.

When the need to breathe finally forced them to break apart slightly, they were both trembling. Brandon gazed down at her, a little afraid of his own overpowering emotions. He had thought he'd lost her. And now that he had her in his arms again, he was all too aware that they had done little more than kiss all week.

"Laura," he groaned, sliding his hands down her back to her bottom so that he could cup her softness and fit her lower body against his.

The intimacy of the embrace pierced through her like a bolt of lightning. She loved this man. And suddenly she was aware as never before of what they might have lost if he hadn't prevented her from leaving for the airport this morning.

She was so choked with feeling that it was all she could do to make her voice work. "Come in the house," she whispered.

As they turned, she saw that in her haste to stop Brandon's departure, she had left the front door wide open. Now it seemed to beckon them to return.

Brandon had pictured the two of them climbing the steps to Laura's bedroom. But they never made it past the living room. Once he had shut the front door and assured their privacy, they came back into each other's arms with a fierce urgency that was almost frightening in its intensity.

She didn't remember afterward whether she unbuttoned her own dress, or who stripped off Brandon's jeans and shirt. But it didn't really matter. The important thing was the exquisite delight of naked flesh arching against naked flesh, the contrasting texture of hair-roughened skin against smooth.

Together they sank down to the soft rug in front of the fireplace. Brandon's lips and hands roamed her body, drawing little cries of joy from the depth of her being. When his questing mouth found her already aroused nipples, she thought she would go up in flames.

Every fiber of her called out for an end to this sweet agony. "Please," she moaned, "don't make me wait any longer."

She felt the weight of his body on top of hers then. He spoke her name, and she twisted against him, begging him to be part of her. He entered her with a fierce possessiveness. And it seemed like only a moment before she felt the first shuddering waves of gratification begin to wash over her.

"Brandon!" His name was on her lips as wave after wave of intense pleasure carried her to an unimaginable crest. And she knew by the shuddering intensity of his release and his half-strangled cry that it had been the same for him.

It was later in the morning, in the warmth of her bed, that they finished the discussion he had begun so much earlier.

"Brandon," she asked almost shyly. "You said you talked to Dr. Grant . . ."

"So you remember that, do you? I thought you weren't listening to anything I was saying."

Laura looked down at her hands, remembering how she had tried to block him out. "I'm sorry I did that to you."

He pulled her closer, stroking his hand across her shoulder and down her arm. "It's all right now. I understand."

For a few moments, neither of them spoke. What if she had driven him away with her stupidity? The thought was too painful to focus on for long.

"What were you trying to tell me about new fertility techniques?" she finally asked in a small voice.

"That there have been a lot of advances in the field. In fact, there's a program at Johns Hopkins Hospital in Baltimore that Dr. Grant says is excellent." He went on to tell her about some of the techniques they were using, including in vitro fertilization. Apparently it had been especially helpful in cases like Laura's.

"Do you think we could go there and try something like that?" she asked excitedly. "I mean, would you be willing to do it?"

Brandon grinned. "It doesn't sound like quite as much fun as the old-fashioned way, but I'd be willing to try whatever you want."

Her eyes shone and she hugged him tightly.

He held her for a moment and then shifted her body so that he could meet her gaze. "However, I think there's one detail you're overlooking. I have the feeling they only accept married couples in that kind of program."

Laura flushed, but her mind was already busy spinning

out plans. "You're right," she mused. "I can't imagine they'd take us until after we got married."

"Does that mean we can get that little detail taken care of soon?" he asked hopefully.

"Yes. I think now *I'm* the one who wants a piece of paper saying you belong to me."

He continued to gaze down into her blue eyes, his expression serious. "And you do understand that, whether we end up having any children or not, this is for keeps. I want to spend the rest of my life with you, Laura Carson. I want to know that you'll be there when I need you. I want to grow old with you."

She nodded, understanding the driving force behind his words. "I want you for keeps too," she assured him, her voice fiercely possessive. "That's why—"

He cut her off. "We're not going to talk about any of that nonsense again."

She hesitated for a moment, understanding why he wanted to put the past behind them. This was a new beginning. But there was one more thing that she had to say, and she suspected it was a subject he wouldn't want to discuss. "Brandon," she finally began, "don't be too hard on your mother. Okay?"

When his features darkened, she went on quickly, "She thought she was doing the right thing. And anyway, what she told me wouldn't have had any effect if I hadn't had my own doubts."

She could see his hand knot into a fist. "Laura, maybe you're right. Now that I'm not so furious anymore, I can see that Jason's death must have affected her more than I realized. She loved that little boy too. And she loved being his grandmother. But if you hadn't come back to me, I don't think I could have ever forgiven her for what she tried to do to you."

"But I came to my senses. And what we have now is much stronger, Brandon. I don't have any more doubts. No matter what life brings us, we will be together."

He hugged her close to his body again, but Laura

wasn't about to drop the issue she had brought up. "If I'm willing to put what your mother did behind me, you have to be too."

Brandon shook his head. "There aren't many women who would be as forgiving as you," he whispered.

"I can afford to be. I know I have your love," she answered, drawing back slightly and smiling up at him confidently.

He held her tightly, letting her know just how strong that love was. And then his lips found hers in an all-consuming kiss that held as much promise of future happiness as present passion.

Epilogue

Laura stood at the open window of her office looking out at the paths that wound through the carefully tended gardens that surrounded Carson's. It was late spring, and the azaleas were a blaze of vivid pinks and reds. But it wasn't the flowers, beautiful though they were, that held her attention. She was watching a tall, dark-haired man who had just turned the corner of a walkway leading toward her. He was chasing a laughing toddler whose dark hair and eyes were remarkably like his own.

The little girl glanced back over her shoulder to make sure that her daddy was following. When she saw that he was almost upon her, she giggled and sped up. Fondly Laura watched the familiar scene, seeing the merriment, and also the love, in the man's eyes as he let his daughter elude his grasp.

As though he knew she was observing the scene, Brandon looked toward the window. When his eyes met Laura's, he grinned and waved.

"Come on out and help me corral your daughter," he called.

"What, and spoil your fun?"

When the little girl heard her mother's voice, she stopped and peered up at the window. "Jessie want Mommy come play tag wid us," she said.

"Yes, come play tag wid us," Brandon laughed.

"Mommy has work to do, Jessica," Laura protested. But even as she spoke, she knew she was going to go out and join the game. Since the birth of her daughter almost two years earlier, she'd turned over more of the responsibility at Carson's to Sylvia and had even hired another landscape architect to take over much of the design work. Although Laura had known that she and Brandon would be happy together no matter what, Jessica was very precious to both of them. Getting pregnant had meant seeing a fertility specialist on a regular basis—and following doctor's orders to the letter. But watching father and daughter together made Laura acutely aware once again that it had all been worth it.

Brandon gave his wife a quick hug as she stepped out into the spring sunshine. Then a small hand tugging on the fabric of her jeans captured her attention. Jessica giggled again and darted off. Together father and mother followed the little girl up and down the paths, always letting her slip from their grasp at the last second.

The game brought forth squeals of delight, and Sylvia came out to see what was provoking all the laughter.

"You're going to wear that child out," she protested.

Brandon paused and gave their friend a conspiratorial wink. "That's the idea. Another fifteen minutes of this and there's going to be no problem with afternoon nap time," he whispered.

"Come play, Aunt Sylvia," the little girl demanded, knowing that she now had another willing adult at her beck and call.

"Well, just for a few minutes."

As the older woman and the child darted off, Brandon turned to his wife and grinned wolfishly. "Want to come home with us for an afternoon siesta? All this running around ought to be good for a two-hour nap at least." The look in his eye told her that he didn't exactly have sleeping in mind for the two of them.

Laura shook her head. "I thought you might have an ulterior motive. And yes, as a matter of fact, I was hoping some handsome man would come along and ask if I was interested in an afternoon nap."

"Any handsome man?" he asked her playfully.

She looked up into the face of the man she had married—the man she loved so much. "No," she whispered, "just you, Brandon. Just you."

EYE OF THE STORM

MAURA SEGER

A powerful portrayal of the events of World War II in the Pacific, *Eye of the Storm* is a riveting story of how love triumphs over hatred. In this, the first of a three book chronicle, Army nurse Maggie Lawrence meets Marine Sgt. Anthony Gargano. Despite military regulations against fraternization, they resolve to face together whatever lies ahead.... Also known by her fans as Laurel Winslow, Sara Jennings, Anne MacNeil and Jenny Bates, Maura Seger, author of this searing novel, was named by ROMANTIC TIMES as 1984's Most Versatile Romance Author.

At your favorite bookstore in March.

EYE-B-1

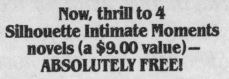

READERS' COMMENTS ON SILHOUETTE DESIRES

"Thank you for Silhouette Desires. They are the best thing that has happened to the bookshelves in a long time."
—V.W.*, Knoxville, TN

"Silhouette Desires—wonderful, fantastic—the best romance around."
—H.T.*, Margate, N.J.

"As a writer as well as a reader of romantic fiction, I found DESIREs most refreshingly realistic—and definitely as magical as the love captured on their pages."
—C.M.*, Silver Lake, N.Y.

"I just wanted to let you know how very much I enjoy your Silhouette Desire books. I read other romances, and I must say your books rate up at the top of the list."
—C.N.*, Anaheim, CA

"Desires are number one. I especially enjoy the endings because they just don't leave you with a kiss or embrace; they finish the story. Thank you for giving me such reading pleasure."
—M.S.*, Sandford, FL

*names available on request